Tales From The Turkey Table

Bill Allman

SHARED VISIONS UNLIMITED

Contents

Foreword by Charles Dickens

These are but shadows of things that could be explained… to a therapist. When I was approached (via Ouija board) to compose a foreword for the treasury of Yuletide wit which you now hold in your hands, my first response was "Oh hell, no!"

After some thought, however, I realized that this was a perfect chance for me to compose one of my legendary run-on sentences and/or run-on paragraphs with which my original works of fiction are replete, essentially as a test of the patience of Victorian readers who, although noted for their long attention spans, were not known for devoting much time to reading given that they were largely illiterate and routinely labouring away in coal mines, steel mills, chimneys for the young ones, and other such places of employment. And I wrote some crackers too: "David Copperfield", "A Tale of Two Cities", "Jaws", and "Great Expectations".

Okay, now that I think about it, I may not have actually written "Jaws", but who's going to argue with a long-dead author? And, of course, I wrote the definitive Christmas ghost story. They even call it "Charles Dickens' A Christmas Carol." As well they should. "A Christmas Carol" went on to become a massive hit and, if I say so myself, a masterpiece.

This collection of "Tales from the Turkey Table" is, by comparison, the ramblings and scribblings of a lesser talent than my own. Some who have read this text have said that Allman has great humour and an incisive satirical wit for Christmas as it SHOULD be, rather than what it is. I say that he merely has a short attention span and the humorous sensibilities of a 14 year old boy. However, I shall allow that this book could put a smile on the face of even the Ghost of Christmas Yet to Come. And that, my friends, would be a sight to see and to never, ever forget. A pleasure which, I can assure you, you will wish had been indefinitely postponed.

Introduction by Bill Allman

Have you grown tired of a certain greeting card company's unending stream of Christmas romance movies? Ever wondered about the mysterious arm stoking the Yule Log fire in the video? Curious about how The Virgin Mary explained her pregnancy to her betrothed, Joseph? And what *does* happen when people get just too carried away by the season?

The answers to these and other questions that you never knew you had lie in the pages of this book.

Oh, and for perfect mulled wine and roast beef with gravy, there are also a pair of recipes to feed your kith and kin through the long winter nights – and get them drunk enough that they will no longer be a bother to you.

Why have I chosen to desecrate Christmas with this collection of off-colour, irreverent Yuletide stories?

Because we've screwed it up. This magical holiday, so captivating for children and meaningful for the religious, has turned into a cartoonish festival of excesses and delusions and I want my piece of the minced meat pie! I may as well join in.

Somewhere along the line, I learned to write.

And somewhere along the line, I learned to enjoy hamburger made from sacred cows.

Here we go.

Happy Christmas to all and to all... turn the page.

A (NOT VERY) HALLMARK CHRISTMAS MOVIE

ACT III

Scene 41 - Ext: Main Street - Night

MUSIC: "I'm Dreaming of a White Christmas" sung by a choir with sleigh bells in the background.

The camera moves from up high in the air down into the small town of Tinsel Grove. Snow graces the rooftops, Christmas lights shine and sparkle on storefronts and houses.

An animatronic Santa Claus waves from the front window of a toy store packed with boats and drums and puzzles and adorable stuffies. The street is skimmed with snow, tire tracks leading to a series of gleaming new pickup trucks and SUVs, all parked by the curbs.

As the camera moves along the main
street, "JAKE'S BAR & GRILLE" appears
at the end of a block.

The camera moves inside as the new,
original Christmas song "Winter is
For Making Love" plays on the jukebox.
The town SANTA CLAUS (it's obvious to
the viewer that it's really kindly,
wise old MR. NORRIS) sits at the bar.

It is warm, it is welcoming. Candles
flicker and a fire glows.

KAYLEIGH, the same 30 year old
brunette that we've been following
through the picture is seated at a
table. She's wearing a much more "down

home" sweater than previously. Gone
are the poser power suits. Her hair
is down. She looks stunning. She
is facing DYLAN, her grade school
crush, handsomely clad in tight
blue jeans, worn work boots, and a
flannel shirt with a plaid pattern
of red and green.

                    KAYLEIGH
(Smiling alluringly) You understand
  that if I follow my heart, I will
give up my apartment in New York for
life here in a farmhouse surrounded
by a babbling brook and our children.

                    DYLAN
I do.

The townspeople in the bar are now
listening to the young couple.

                    KAYLEIGH
(beaming) I like the sound of that.

                    DYLAN
Make my Christmas wish come true.
You were the only one who ever really
                  could.

In the background, MR. NORRIS in his
Santa suit hears this and throws up
his hands in anger.

                  MR. NORRIS
             What the f…!?!

NORRIS jumps off his bar stool and
stomps away to the washroom shaking
his head in disgust.

                  KAYLEIGH
        And there's Jacob. What will I tell
                   Jacob?

                  DYLAN
        Jacob isn't really for you.
        This is where you belong.
           Your home. [beat]
        With your heart-family.

KAYLEIGH doodles a heart out of coffee
sugar on the table. She nods slowly.
Then decides.

                  KAYLEIGH
Here's the thing, Dylan. Jacob makes
   eight hundred thousand dollars a
year, wears tailored Armani suits and
   drives a Porsche. (She looks deeply

s deeply into Dylan's eyes) You sold a kidney to save your grandfather's farm from foreclosure. So this situation… (she indicates the two of them with her hand). Not happening.

DYLAN
But I'm hung like a horse.

KAYLEIGH
See, that's *another* problem Dylan. Why would you even KNOW what a horse is hung like?

Dylan gets down on one knee as the townspeople turn to face him. He fumbles in the pocket of his jeans and pulls out a small red stocking with white fur trim. He holds it out to Kayleigh. Her eyes widen in shock.

KAYLEIGH
What?! (she covers her mouth as the townspeople smile) What's happening?!

DYLAN
Kayleigh, will you make me the merriest man in Tinsel Grove?

Dylan pulls a diamond ring from
the stocking. It glistens in the
firelight as he offers it to Kayleigh.

                    KAYLEIGH
What? But… Dylan. How did you even pay
                    for this?

                     DYLAN
    I sold the other kidney.

Dylan dies.

                    THE END

Away In A Manger

I am not a farmer.

I don't dress like a farmer. I sure as hell don't WORK as hard as a farmer but, more importantly, I absolutely do not keep farmer hours.

Sunrise? I've heard about it. Maybe seen a picture. Stayed up all night to see one, once. Booze was involved.

So, to reiterate, NOT a farmer.

However, I have enough life experience to know which end of a cow to feed. I can ride and groom a horse. And I have climbed through a hedgerow only to come face to face with a very territorial bull. What matters is that I've lived to tell the tale.

And through the years, I've heard the songs and stories about the miracle of the animals being able to speak at the time of the birth of Jesus.

Don't get your hopes up. I've heard the "water to wine" story, too, and let me tell you, THAT is a colossal fraud. Except for the dog on "Family Guy", talking animals are a Bernie Madoff level fraud.

However, I thought that it was kind of sweet when the local United Church decided to host a "real manger" scene on their front lawn. "Meet actual animals" boasted the advert. Being as my neighbourhood is filled with dyed-in-the-wool "city kids", I figured that this was a fantastic way for families to take in the joy of the Christmas season while learning about living, breathing animals. You know? The kind that we rely on because we wear them and eat them.

Now I want a steak. Is Hy's Steakhouse open at 11 o'clock at night?

So it came to pass on a Sunday in late December that a shelter built out of two-by-fours and plywood, complete with a manger and multiple bales of hay, appeared on the lawn of the United Church near my house. I took a look at the construction and am fairly certain that it was built by church folks with circular saws and pneumatic Brad Nailers. Not a rough-hewn timber in sight. St. Joseph must have been on a break.

I returned later in the day to take a look. I was anticipating a volunteer "Holy Family" with the infant Jesus and an age-appropriate Virgin Mary with her betrothed, St. Joseph, standing by.

Nope.

The church folk had clearly put all of their efforts into acquiring the animals. They had not furnished a Holy Family. Instead, they had set out two coat racks full of costumes for people to borrow. There was a blue robe for Mary. There was a rough woolen cloak for Joseph and similar ones for the startled shepherds. There were glitter and glue spangled robes for the Three Kings. And all of these costumes were flapping in the breeze, unloved. But the angels... now there's a different story! Everyone wanted to be an angel, no one present even knew the meaning of the word "virgin", and "Wise Men" sounded like work. And lo, a collection of children aged five, six, and seven who would normally be stuck to their iPads, had gathered at the manger on this cold December afternoon to marvel at the miracle of the birth of Jesus — as presented by the United Church. As presented without Jesus, Mary, or Joseph. But at least they had the donkey that took them all to Bethlehem. And the stable.

Two calves, two goats, a sheep, and a donkey were surrounded by a shifty-looking gaggle of children all wearing flowing white robes, hideous tinsel and wire hanger haloes, and fake wings trimmed with real (but moulting) feathers. As the angels wandered around the compound, they left behind a veritable cloud of white feathers. It honestly looked as if some bored hunter had taken to target practicing on the Heavenly Host.

While the well-meaning and kind-hearted church folk had capably set up an enclosure to keep the animals close to the baby Jesus's manger, they had not thought through the jumping capability of nervous farm animals.

Particularly sheep.

Just as I stepped from my car, the lone sheep in the manger scene looked at the three foot high fence and decided to book it for freedom. Sheep can really jump when they want to. I was the closest one to the stable (and likely the only one who had ever actually herded sheep), so I sprinted after the sheep and, for a few moments, a foot chase worthy of a 70s cop show unfurled on Main Street. I gained on the sheep and seized him by the scruff of his neck and his backside. Lifting him up, I marched him back to the trailer in which he had arrived. A church person stepped forward and opened the gate (sheepishly). I gently tossed the getaway inside and the door swung shut behind him.

I looked at the church person, SO earnest in his demeanor, and promptly demanded to know: "Where are the shepherds? The book says there were shepherds. Sheep on the loose, not a shepherd in sight." Then I added, I thought under my breath: "Fuck."

Apparently, I am not as quiet as I thought I was. Also, apparently, the book prohibits saying "fuck" because the church person turned white and covered his ears.

Goddamnit.

The excitement over, people turned their attention back to the manger scene brought to you by the United Church and an overbooked hotel two thousand years ago.

The manger scene, still lacking a Holy Family, had devolved into an Orwellian animal farm and some goats, let me tell you, are more equal than others. Because there, in the manger itself, in the crib supposedly occupied by our Lord and Saviour, a lone goat had climbed up and was resting, contentedly chewing on some hay and wondering why a host of angels were making such a fuss over him. I'm confident that months later, Baby Goat Jesus would be crucified and served in a delicious curry sauce.

But, for today, King of the Goats was Lord of the Stable.

And the children were, indeed, entranced. Most had never been up close to a farm animal of any kind, and now, clad in dollar store angel costumes, a multitude of the little dears were "oohing" and "ahhing" over the spectacle before them. What the church people had created was probably as close to a Middle Eastern barn as could be created in a Pacific Northwest rain forest.

But it must not be lost on us that, despite their definite devotion to celebrating what they perceived as the "true" meaning of Christmas, the good, kind church people knew jack shit about animals.

Animals shit, animals fart. Children (even angels) are not silent about these matters. And so, instead of a chorus of voices crying out "hark" or "fear not", a half dozen wee ones intoned "That one just pooped out of his bum bum!" and "Ewww, donkey made a doody!", as well

as "Cow farts! Cow farts!" which was accompanied by
excited pointing and hand waving.

I suppose that it was
an excess of excitement,
and there may have been
too much sugar, but
one of the little angels
(literally, one of the angels)
turned, panic-stricken to
her mother and said, in
a not-so-heavenly voice,
"Mommy, I don't feel well".
As the angel clutched her
tummy, mom rifled through her purse until she found
a bag. The angel sat down, heavily, on a log and mom
handed her the bag which she promptly filled with vomit.

The bag was clear plastic.

The visual alone set off another angel and an "Exorcist"
quality stream of vomit bounced off one of the cows.
The cow promptly dropped a cow flop out of its arse.
The acrid odour of angel vomit mixed with cow shit
reached the noses of three other angels at the same time.
And suddenly there appeared on the lawn, a heavenly
host of hurling angels, gagging, retching, and projectile
vomiting. Even the animals were disgusted. The donkey
moved away from the burgeoning scene, anxious to press
himself into a far corner. And, let's be honest, when
it comes to foul stenches, donkeys have no moral high
ground.

This is the point at which I turned away. The chaos unfolding was less reminiscent of the Gospel of Luke and more like the Book of Revelations.

One Christmas later, the United Church rented an antique sleigh and offered pictures with Santa.

Even family pets were excluded.

The Virgin Mary's Letter

Mary, Daughter of Joachim
Nazareth, Galilee
1613101

March 26, 0 BC

Dearest Joseph,

First of all, thank you SO much for the absolutely lovely offer of marriage. After much thought, reflection (and, to please you, prayer), I most graciously accept. Yes. I will be your bride. Mrs. Carpenter. I do so like the sound of that. It's not so clunky as "Mrs. Son of Jacob" and besides, I think that as time goes on, there will be many, many famous Jewish carpenters. Working with tools just seems very... *Hebrew* to me.

We have a few hurdles to overcome. First, we're not related. That really isn't done now, is it Joe? I mean, look at the story of Adam and Eve. They have Cain, they have Abel, but Cain kills Abel. The book never mentions any sisters (gross) and it doesn't seem that any of the offspring were too inbred, and yet there's not a whole lot of, you know, CHOICE when it comes to mates. Anyway, all I'm saying is that there's precedent for relatives hooking up. I think that the original book of Exodus read "And Adam and Eve begat Cain and Abel who begat a long line of banjo players." But that's not what this is about.

Joe, we have an age difference. I'm 15. You're 90. You're older than my father's father's father. And yet, it doesn't bother me. I have read prophecy that ageing musicians will one day marry teenaged girls and prophecy is never wrong, now is it? Nonetheless, it doesn't bother me one bit. And I suppose for you it's better when you make a commitment like "til death do us part" that "'til death" shouldn't be all that far off, right?

Now, we need to talk about family, Joseph. Naturally, I understand that you're wanting to procreate, to see your lineage carried on. Let me be frank, Joe. At 90, your little swimmers aren't going to be winning any Olympic medals (it's a Greek thing) and that's assuming that there's even any spring left in the diving board.

90.

But I know how important this is to you. AND I know how important your faith is to you. And, remember, I said that I'd been praying a lot, so it's your faith that I'd like to address. Um, Joe, you know your prophets, right? Do you remember crazy old Isaiah from Jerusalem? I mean, I know you don't REMEMBER him... he lived about 700 years ago (although, you're 90, maybe you did know him, LOL). Well, I was madly flipping through Isaiah's writings the other day and I found the most interesting passage. Here it is:

For unto us a child is born, unto us a son is given: and the government shall be upon his shoulder: and his name shall be called Wonderful, Counsellor, The mighty God, The everlasting Father, The Prince of Peace.

That's kind of a mouthful if you ask me. But the point of it is this: G-d is going to give the world a SON! A baby. I mean, it says "son", but it could be a daughter, we don't know. Really, girls can do anything boys can do... except vote, hold property, read scripture. There's nothing that says the Messiah can't be a girl, right? I mean, not likely. At least no more than 50% likely.

So, I read this chapter... I know, I know, I'm not supposed to read scripture, but I had some time and the Galilee Herald is sending out the prophecies in serialized form. With every clay jug of milk, you get a new chapter. And I've been getting regular milk deliveries. So I read. And there's this bit. And I think "Well, who's the lucky stiff who gets to be the Messiah's father?"

Please don't take "stiff" personally. It's a figure of speech.

But I had other things to do. Clothing to smack with a stick, wheat to flail, water to carry, and I thought no more about it until the end of the day when I went to sleep.

I was lying on the floor of my mother and father's hovel, when a glorious light shone down upon me and I woke up. I started to curse the glare. Honestly Joe, I said some really un-devout things. I mean I turned the air in that room as blue as my favourite robe. But that's beside the point. I think I called one of G-d's angels a C***. Which, in Hebrew, is actually the "gimel" word. Well, Gabriel (that's what he said his name was) got over it. I guess when you're an angel, you need to have thick skin. And he went on to tell me that the MOTHER of the Son of G-d was going to be ME! ME! Joseph, little old virginal ME!

I argued. I said "But Gabe" (I call him Gabe, we got on really well) "But Gabe," I said, "I am a virgin and have never known man." And Gabriel said "The Holy Ghost shall come upon thee…"

And I stopped him, because even a virgin knows that THAT ain't how conception works. But he went on "and the power of the most High shall overshadow thee." Okay, a little domination, I can deal with that. Paying attention to this, Joe? "And therefore also the Holy which shall be born of thee shall be called the Son of God."

Honestly, Joe, I kind of started to nod off around there. He went on about my cousin Elizabeth, who got knocked up when she was 88 years old. Again, just gotta say… *gross*. The first thing out of that baby's mouth is going to be a big coughing, crying cloud of dust.

After Gabe had delivered his shtick, I asked him "So, are you done?" Which, given the subject matter, seemed like the right thing to say. And Gabe said "Yep, done." And then he left. From what my non-virgin friends tell me, this is pretty much standard operating procedure. In any event, I went to sleep, and I guess during the night the Holy Ghost visited me and did his dirty business because in the morning, I woke up pregnant... with G-d's child!

Cool, right?

Of course right.

Now, there are some serious upsides to this, Joe. First, G-d's child. I'm thinking that our years of waiting for a table in a restaurant or a room at the inn are over! The other upside is that, at least until the Messiah is born, I'm done with my monthlies! Also cool because, under Hebrew law, I've been having to shag off and separate from everyone for a week while I bleed. And, of course, I haven't been able to use any of my parents' or friends' furniture because I'll make it "unclean". What rubbish.

But, what I know is going to thrill you beyond words, this is prophecy coming true and we're right at the centre of it! I know, I know. People are going to talk. You'll have friends who say that I'm just some broad who got knocked up and saw you as a safe landing spot. But really, Joe, why would I lie about this? I mean, no offense, but you're a carpenter. It's not like you're sitting on a thousand yokes of land or have some awesome job with the Roman occupation government with a big salary and a sweet pension.

I mean, you could. And I suppose a more ambitious man might, but you do you, Joe. It's nice that you've found a good Jewish girl to marry. At 90.

Darling Joseph, I am happy beyond words that the Lord has chosen to bless us, to pick US for this most monumental miracle. We are going to be the parents of the world's Saviour, of the Messiah!

We'll have a child who will be loved by everyone, who will be popular beyond belief, and who will be able to look after us into our old age. I don't know for sure what "Messiah" pays, but I bet that it's a lot.

Well, I'd best sign off now. It's almost milk delivery time!

Love,

(still the virgin) Mary

CHRISTMAS MUSIC

On November 13, 2017, somewhere between the Palmolive and the Drano at an unnamed grocery store, the sound system began playing "Santa Claus is Coming to Town".

And I snapped.

I rolled my buggy, laden sleigh-like, with bottles of Diet Coke and cartons of 2% milk, up to the cashier. "YOU KNOW THAT YOU'RE BEING PSYCHOLOGICALLY ABUSED, DON'T YOU?!?" I screamed. This only seemed to further unsettle her. But she nodded, "I know. It gets earlier every year. There's even been a study."

I had heard of the study. It's actually not a study. It's an opinion posited by British counselling psychologist Linda Blair. I'd have changed my name rather than being mistaken for the star of "The Exorcist", but at least she always has a reason to vomit in public. "My counsellor puked on me!" "Ach, that's okay, it's Linda Blair." When working as a counselling psychologist, best to come to work drunk to the point of gastric distress, I say.

I continued to the clerk. "Do you know Eric Idle's 'Fuck Christmas'?" I asked. "Know it? I LOVE IT!" she responded eagerly. Michael Buble began pouring out of the speakers with "Christmas (Baby Please Come Home)" and I rocked back and forth like Dustin Hoffman in "Rain Man"... but without the inappropriate touching. Finally slowing down, I peered up at the speakers, hung from a pipe 20 feet in the air like Big Brother's loudhailers from "1984". New slogan: "Big Brother Wishes You and Yours the Best of the Holiday Season".

"Want me to rip those down?" I asked.

"Sure, I'll go get the ladder," replied the clerk, enthusiastically.

"I don't need a ladder," I said. "Be right back."

I pushed my way down the soft drink aisle past a dozen zombified customers all searching for an environmentally friendly pancreatic cancer agent. Finally, I found the Holy Grail. Ginger beer. In glass bottles. I returned to the front of the store with a dozen under my arm and found a shopping buggy. In truth, I took the shopping buggy away from an octogenarian in a red and green jumper. With a grocery-spilling heave, I turned that fucker on its back and stood atop. "I THROW THIS BOTTLE IN THE NAME OF... AHHH, WHATEVER!"

And with that, I swung back and hurled the glass projectile right at the nearest speaker. It struck the grille and smashed with a satisfying spray of glass and carbonated drink. The clerk stripped off her smock and screamed "DEATH TO CAROLS!" which, in hindsight, served to do little except freak out the three customers in the store whose names were actually Carol. They all fled and I flung another bottle at the speakers. Another splintery splash and the rig swung to and fro. Buble's voice warbled a little.

Another bottle, and this time the grille fell off the closest cabinet, tearing out the guts of the speaker as it fell to the floor. Buble persisted. "And all the fun we had last ye-ear…" One speaker left. I lined up the shot and threw as hard as I could. By now, the clerk had torn apart her black employee golf shirt and was standing in only her bra and work pants waving her arms over her head and shrieking like one of Jane Goodall's study subjects. This bottle snapped in two on the pipe holding the speakers. They swayed. Another bottle, a direct hit on the final speaker, and "Christmas! The snow's coming do-own…" were the last words heard on the public address system. What was coming down was the entire 40 pound speaker rig. Straight into a pyramid of Coca-Cola, all faced with Jolly Old St. Nicholas enjoying his soda pop of choice.

The explosion of Coke foam, speaker parts, and wires merely whipped the clerk and me into a further frenzy. I leapt from the top of the overturned buggy and dashed to the aisle containing lighter fluid. Running back with an armload of bottles marked "Extremely Flammable", I screamed to the clerk: "FIRE! MUST! HAVE! FIRE!"

She responded with primal
urgency and, as I tore lid
after lid from the lighter
fluid bottles, emptying their
contents onto the mass of
sound gear and aluminum
cans, she lit an entire book
of matches and threw it
into the fray. With a sudden

"whoompf", the fireball reached the ceiling, attracting
the attention of the store's night manager.

"What the fuck is going on?!?" he screamed as he ran up
to the conflagration.

"CHRISTMAS MUSIC! CHRISTMAS MUSIC
TOO SOON!" shrieked the clerk. "JINGLE BELLS!
JINGLE BELLS! SANTA CLAUS ROASTING ON
AN OPEN FIRE! WE WISH YOU A MERRY
MELLONFARMING CHRISTMAS!"

The manager stood, staring at his half-naked employee
who then began to sing: "DECK THE HALLS
WITH PARTS OF MOLLY, FA-LA-LA-LA-LA,
LA-LA-LA-LA. 'TIS THE SEASON TO BE
LOADED, FA-LA-LA-LA-LA, LA-LA-LA-LA!"

The manager slowly removed his name tag and stared
down at it. DICK WETHERALL (not his real name),
MANAGER, it read. He squinted and tossed the tag
into the flaming pyre in front of him. "I didn't sign up
for this shit." he said quietly, unbuttoning his shirt.

When I left the store, there they were, the clerk
and the store manager, locked in an unholy embrace,
dancing naked around the flaming mass of particle
board, aluminum, and food store uniform clothing. Some
customers ran to their cars, some stripped off and joined
in, others watched, agog, recording the incident on their
phones for Facebook posterity. No one said a word as I
crossed the parking lot and climbed into my SUV. Not
a sound could be heard save for the shrieks, grunts, and
sizzles from inside the store as the fire spread into the
cheese display.

An elderly woman near my car peered into the store. "Oh,
why did they have to shut off the Christmas songs? I do
like them so much."

I turned up a Nirvana CD and backed over the old bat and
her walker.

Then I drove away into the night.

The Man Behind The Poker

"Wear the shirt." she purred from the bedroom. I sighed and pulled on the green flannel. Feeling now like an object rather than a celebrity, I stepped into my room. My jeans lay on the floor in a ball, my "tighty whities" tossed carelessly onto my dresser. "Get me naked" she'd gasped only minutes earlier. Then she stopped. "But wear the shirt."

The shirt. That Goddamned shirt.

You've all seen the "Yule Log" video. You know, the one that runs for like six straight hours and shows a couple of logs burning in a fireplace while terrible covers of classic Christmas songs leak out of your television speakers. That video costs broadcasters about 10 dollars a day. A piece of shit Christmas movie starring rejects from the cast of "Saved By the Bell" costs at least a few thousand. So, on

Christmas Day, when ad revenues are lower than a legless reindeer's dick, guess which program wins out.

And if you recall that video, you'll remember that about every 20 minutes, some anonymous arm in a green flannel shirt reaches in with an iron fireplace poker and rearranges the flaming logs so that they burn more brightly. About every second time this happens, the stranger adds another log to the pyre.

I'm that stranger.

I'm the guy in the green flannel shirt.

I am the man behind the poker.

More people have seen my arm than have seen all the "Star Wars" movies. I did the research. I looked at the numbers. That fucking fire has been shown in no less than two hundred countries and it runs, on average, for 72 hours per year. Not to mention downloads, DVD sales, and, back when Christ was a kid, VHS copies. Yep, home videos would blow off store shelves by the thousands at 5:59 on Christmas Eve when dum-as-fuk husbands realized that they had forgotten to get their wives any presents. And if you're a dum-as-fuk husband, and if you DON'T get your wife a present, well then you'd better become a Goddamned yoga master because your only chance at oral gratification on Christmas Eve will be self-administered.

And how did I get to be the most famous arm in the world? Well, to understand that journey, we need to go back to the 1980s. It was a time of material excess. Ronald Reagan was in the White House and "Trickle Down" economics was either being derided as fiscal fantasy or celebrated as a new Gospel. And all over America, people were finding new and ridiculous ways to spend money. A few years earlier, it had been the pet rock. Rocks. Actual rocks in boxes that sold for actual money. The guy who invented pet rocks was worth TWO MILLION DOLLARS.

Let that sink in. TWO mil. He died in 2015. Sadly, he did not die by being stoned to death in an Abu Dhabi prison. That would have been good for a collective little giggle from a nation that felt maybe they'd been lead into one massive economic kick in the nuts.

But, two million dollars. Good for him.

So, it's the 1980s and my buddy Leonard produced porn. A graduate of Pasadena Film Academy, class of 1974, he'd hacked around Hollywood trying to land a gig on a movie. Then he tried for a movie of the week, then a sitcom, then a commercial, then a community service station. Everywhere he turned, it came up shit. Nobody was hiring. Well, that's not true. If he'd graduated from UCLA Film School, by the 1980s he'd have been sipping Mai Tais with Spielberg and refusing my phone calls.

But Pasadena's tuition was cheaper by a lousy three hundred bucks.

Putz.

And, so there we were in 1982, in a fake Irish bar in Burbank. We were knocking back the Guinness and I was paying. I was the only one of us who was employed, albeit at a local bookstore. Still, it was a job "in the arts", so I was feeling pretty proud of myself! I was even thinking that I'd be getting off graveyard shift that month and getting to meet actual customers.

And that's when Leonard said "I think I'll produce porn."

"HUH?" I yelped.

"Porn," he reiterated. "There's a big scene up the Valley right now, anyone can break in. And I've got an awesome 16mm camera, my own lights, and an edit suite."

"And no food." I reminded him.

"And no food." he repeated. "Porn it is."

For the next year, Leonard produced porn. He filmed magnificent scenes of men with women, women with men, two men with one woman, two women with one man. And a goat. If it could fit into a human orifice, then Leonard exposed top-quality motion picture celluloid capturing it. He filmed tongues, fingers, penises, sex toys, fruit, pop bottles. If anyone had thought of it, he'd have filmed cigars, too. But we were a decade away from having a Democrat in the White House.

"When are you going to release a film?" I'd ask. His friends would ask. His mother thought that he worked in the Burbank Library. So she didn't ask.

But Leonard was resolute. "I'm building up a catalogue" he'd boast. "The Beatles did this. They'd record, like FIVE albums over a weekend and then go on tour so that an album could be released every month." I didn't bother to check his information. In hindsight, someone really should have.

But by the end of that year, Leonard had no less than 18 full-length feature pornographic motion pictures shot and edited with soundtracks added, ready to go on sale to any one of 30 distributors of premium adult entertainment. He had maxed out all his credit cards, and his parents', and mine. He had spent a fortune in production, but was confident that he would recoup the same and more.

And then VHS came along.

Time and again, Leonard endured the same meeting. He would stride into a distributor's office, proudly place a can of film on the desk, and pitch the product inside with near-religious fervour. "THIS! THIS is sex as America wants it! Wild, free, rough, gentle, ethnic, and sometimes kinky. Production values that rival most Oscar winners! And the exclusive rights to it can be yours for only five thousand dollars. Per state."

And each time the distributor would look him squarely in the eye and say: "I can buy 15 hours of teens humping in hot tubs - worldwide rights, in perpetuity, on home video for a thousand bucks."

After which the meeting would dissolve. Sometimes the distributor would say "Now get the fuck out." Sometimes, it was just implied.

Back at the fake Irish bar in Burbank, a year after his fateful decision, Leonard was despondent. I, however, was now third assistant manager at the bookstore, so I was feeling pretty flush with cash. We sat on stools in front of the surly bartender drinking copious amounts of rum and eggnog. Leonard later confessed that he was contemplating whether hanging himself would hurt for very long. I was staring absent-mindedly at the blurry television screen hanging over the bottles that proclaimed to be Jameson Irish Whiskey. In actual fact, the same bottles had graced the shelves of that fake Irish bar for years. By the time Leonard and I settled there on that December night, the bottles were filled with a mixture of water (30%), tea for colouring (10%), and locally distilled Irish poitin (60%). Made in a garage from potatoes, even one shot of the acidic Irish moonshine known as poitin, or potcheen, or potheen can blind any human. But mixed with water, tea, and a base of cola - at eight bucks each - the blindness is generally temporary.

The impotence, however, can be eternal.

Leonard was babbling. "I have four thousand feet of unexposed film left." he moaned.

"Uh-huh." I replied, not listening. I motioned to the bartender to refill my glass of rum and eggnog from the punch bowl.

"I got a killer deal on roll ends from Fuji. I mean, the stock is probably five years old. But I only paid a buck a foot."

Still, I wasn't listening. (Turns out, he left this information in the first draft of his suicide note from which I was able to copy each detail.)

I kept staring at the screen over the bar. I slapped Leonard.

"Look at that!" I exclaimed. "A burning log. Who the fuck watches a burning log?"

Leonard screwed up his face. "What the fuck?" he slurred. "When did that start?"

I knew this one. When you work graveyards in a bookstore, you read a lot of useless shit. Still, I felt pretty clever because I KNEW THIS ONE!!!!

Leonard scooped his glass into the punchbowl, simultaneously filling it, polluting the bowl, and spilling rum and eggnog all over the bar.

"I KNOW THIS!" I blurted. And here's what I know:

The "Yule Log" film was created in New York for station WPIX in 1966. It was ordered by the CEO of WPIX as a "gift" to the people of New York and to his employees. Running it on Christmas Eve meant that his workforce could all go home and spend time with their families. I wonder how many workers counted that as a "gift".

Anyway, the original loop was on 16mm film, was only 17 seconds long, and was filmed at Gracie Mansion, the official residence of the Mayor of New York City. Before filming, a crew person decided to remove the wire fireplace screen to allow better viewing of the crackling blaze. Of course, a large ember burst out from the chimney and right onto the City's $4,000.00 antique rug and burned a hole into it. So there's that budget out of control. There was no clear record of whether WPIX had to pay for the rug (I'm certain they did) but the decision to run the film on Christmas Eve cost *the station $4,000.00 in ad revenue. And a new rug. And 17 seconds of film, as well as production costs.*

By 1969, the original film was falling apart (film does that) so WPIX decided to film yet another blazing Yule Log Christmas extravaganza. For some reason, the New York Mayor's Office told them to piss off, so they relocated their filming to the land where all great movies are made... California.

Out in LA-LA Land, a fireplace with similar metalwork to the Mayor's was found and a high value 35mm movie was made one hot August afternoon - six minutes and three seconds of a roaring fireplace. Lovely. Perfect. Boring.

Leonard and I sat at the bar staring up at the flickering images on the screen. The WPIX original selection of carols and Christmas jingles blared out from the sound system. We watched as one log burned out and collapsed onto the other. We watched as both logs slid down through the grate. Then we watched as the image on the screen jumped and, suddenly, both logs were whole and blazing again. After the third round of disappointment, Leonard looked at me.

"I could do better than that." he mused.

"Sure you could, buddy!" I replied. "But why would you want to?"

"Ever seen a goat naked?" he asked.

"Nope. Yes. Maybe. I don't know."

"People can't be deceived any longer." he said. "The people want realism. They want warmth. They want to experience a total Christmas aesthetic, not just a trite image of wood burning."

I had a job in the arts. I understood the word "trite".

"You have the film." I reminded him.

"And you have the camera."

Leonard jolted upright in his seat, renewed enthusiasm coursing through his eggnog-clogged arteries.

"I'm making a movie!" he declared at full volume. "And then I'll transfer it to VHS, sell 10 million copies, and die in a cocaine-fuelled sex orgy!"

"With a goat." I added.

"NO MORE GOATS!" hollered Leonard.

Two weeks later in a palatial home in Orange County, Leonard's camera sat on a tripod facing a giant stone fireplace with a pile of birch and some newspaper kindling stacked up and ready to be set ablaze. Leonard was staking everything on this epic and he paced as he pondered every cinematic detail. He had eight different crew members on "set". One person handled the tripod, one was a film magazine loader for the camera, one was a gaffer (which Leonard explained to me was "pro talk" for an electrician), one was a key grip (responsible for lighting), one was a best boy gaffer (head assistant to the gaffer), one was a best boy grip (head assistant to the key grip), one was a director of photography/camera operator, and one was responsible for "slating" the production using a clapper board to mark the scene and take of each shot. In addition to these people, Leonard was the director and had cast me as "talent".

"Talent?" I asked when he proposed the notion to me.

"Sure!" he said. "I was going over the storyboard last night..."

"The what?"

"The storyboard. It's a collection of drawings that set out the director's vision for..."

"I know what a storyboard is. I just didn't imagine that you'd use one for shooting a single image of a burning log in a fireplace."

"Oh, I got a great deal on the panels." he reassured me. "I got the same guy who drew for "Jaws... Two"."

Oh God.

"So, here's what you do." he continued. "When I say "ACTION!", you light up the fire. Then you watch the fire burn. And we're burning, burning, burning. Then when I call "POKER IN!", you move your arm into frame right with the fireplace poker, and you prod the logs around so that they burn more brightly. Then you step back and wait. Pick up another log and be ready to go. And now we're burning, burning, burning. When I say "LOG IN!" you move your arm into frame right, drop the log you're holding onto the fire, and then use the poker to straighten it out."

No problem.

"First setup ready?" called Leonard. The crew looked at him. The director of photography, a man in his 60s with a wealth of high and low budget experience behind him, smiled and spoke effusively. "All ready, sir!" The grips and gaffers and loader and clapper all nodded mutely. Leonard was pleased and looked to me. "Got it?"

I was missing something. "Yeah, but I need…"

"RIGHT!" said Leonard. "We never talked about your motivation."

For the next 10 minutes I stood, unable to interrupt him, while Leonard expounded all the reasons why my "character" would want to stoke a fire.

"Maybe," he mused, "this is the fire that's keeping him alive in the mountains. Or maybe it's the fire that warmed the manger where the Baby Jesus lay."

He finally had to breathe in, so I interrupted.

"I need matches."

"Oh." said Leonard.

There were no matches in the home. So we all waited for 30 minutes while the best boy grip ran to a nearby corner store to purchase a pack of matches. He returned – at a walk - to the set, passing by the gaffers out on the sidewalk enjoying cigarettes – ignited with their Bic lighters.

Break over, the crew returned to their places. The best boy grip handed me the pack of matches. Leonard yelled "PLACES!" and a variety of voices cried out filmy stuff like "Lamp on!" and "Standing by!"

The gaffer looked over from his place leaning on a light stand as I fumbled with the matchbook.

"You got a pyro license?" he inquired. I stopped and stared at him.

"Handling fire effects, you're supposed to have a licensed pyrotechnics technician on set." he growled at Leonard.

Leonard was speechless.

"But I'll let it slide with a 10% unsafe workspace premium tacked onto everyone's fees."

The director of photography smiled, "That's actually really fair, John," he reassured Leonard, who smiled tensely and nodded.

"Roll camera!" said Leonard.

"Rolling!" barked the director of photography.

"Aaaaaaaand... ACTION!" called Leonard. I struck a match. It went out. I tossed the dead match into the hearth and struck a second one. It took and the flame burned brightly in my hand as I bent and touched it to the newspaper. The fire caught, and I moved the match to three other points, lighting up the paper in each one to ensure that the pyre would ignite properly.

On Leonard's urging, I stepped back and watched with pride. Within a minute, there was a roaring fire filling the fireplace. Leonard watched the scene through his director's viewfinder and looked to the director of photography who spent the entire time staring intently through the camera's eyepiece, periodically giving a "thumbs up" whenever he knew that Leonard was watching him.

Leonard stood, intently watching the flames and muttering "And we're burning... burning... good... keep burning. Nice."

Within about 20 minutes, the fire was beginning to die down. Leonard looked to me and indicated the poker. "Fire's dying down," he cooed. "Baby Jesus is getting cold. It's all on you to make it better."

I picked up the poker, extended my arm into the fireplace, and pushed the logs around so that unburnt wood was exposed. The fire blazed back to life and Leonard waved me out of the shot. "Good, good." he intoned. "Now just stand there and be... reverent."

"And we're burning... burning... good... keep burning. Nice."

The fire began to fade once again. Leonard motioned to me to pick up another piece of wood.

"Standby extra log." he said.

"Log standing by!" I replied.

Leonard continued, half-whispering and very solemn: "Now remember, this log is going to feed the fire, to warm the stable. It's not just any log. It could be wood that was cut by Saint Joseph the Carpenter, Mary's betrothed. Be ready. Standby. Aaaaand…" Then he yelled out: "ADD LOG! ACTION! ACTION!"

I reached into the shot, dropped the log into the fire, and then used the poker to move the burning bits of wood around to what I judged to be aesthetically pleasing positions. "Nice." said Leonard, wiping away a tear.

For almost two hours, we endured changing film magazines, new logs, a burnt-out lamp, and two tantrums from Leonard, who felt that I wasn't being sufficiently reverent while offscreen.

When it was done, the crew packed up the equipment and turned over their labour invoices. Leonard paid them with a stack of cheques, and then piled the cans of exposed film into his Datsun hatchback. He insisted on hugging each one of the crew members, thanking them profusely for being part of his "vision".

After they'd all gone, he turned to face me. "Thanks for believing." he said. Before I could respond, he wrapped his arms around me and held me until it became uncomfortable.

I saw very little of Leonard for the next few months. And then, one day in November, he called me.

"I SOLD IT! I SOLD IT!" he screamed into the phone.

"Sold what? The Datsun? About time." I replied.

"NO! The 'Yule Log' film. International buyer! Televised distribution! Home video marketing in EVERY major retail outlet in America!"

"Yeah. And?"

"I'M RICH!!!!" he screamed. "The advance alone cleared up my entire debt load!"

"Well, except for my credit cards…" I started, but he was already away and rambling.

"PLUS, I get a royalty from each copy sold and each broadcast made."

"Hey, that's great." I responded, unenthusiastically.

"And I'm giving you 10%, buddy! You earned it."

"Well, that's not so bad. But about my credit cards…"

"We'll get to that." he assured me.

And Leonard was as good as his word. He paid me back and, on December 17th of that year, threw a party in our favourite fake Irish bar. He invited the crew, his parents, and a long list of people he perceived as "celebrities". Mostly, that list consisted of various background performers and bit players, the sort whose career highlight is playing "Man in Phone Booth" or "Corpse in Morgue" on a detective show.

None of them showed up.

Although Leonard had expected to close out the bar for a "private function", the owner looked at him and snorted "Close the bar? A week before Christmas? Not for all the cocaine in Hollywood, and certainly not for two hundred bucks in guaranteed liquor sales."

So, we carried on with the party. Crew members and family mixed with the usual array of fake Irish bar regulars. At about nine pm, Leonard tried to make a speech. The owner yelled at him to "KEEP IT DOWN!" And then the owner ran the "Yule Log" video on the TV above the bar. He sort of had to. Leonard had given him an autographed "director's copy" of the VHS. Nobody knew that Leonard had bought the VHS tape at the local 7-11, torn the plastic wrap off, and signed it with a Sharpie on his way to the bar.

I sat on a stool at the bar, watching the video as a weak arrangement of "Have Yourself a Merry Little Christmas" played out of the TV speakers. I chuckled when I saw my own arm come into the frame, poker in hand, and push the burning logs around. And I jumped when Leonard yelled at the top of his lungs: "AND THAT'S HIM!!! THAT'S THE MOST FAMOUS ARM IN THE WORLD!!!". He pointed at me and I faced the rest of the bar, frozen. After a brief, and intensely awkward, stare-off with the other party guests, I smiled, waved, and turned back to the bar, sliding my suit jacket through a puddle of stale Guinness.

I became aware of someone standing beside me. She was a redhead with a full, killer body. I glanced at her, and then refocused my attention on the TV. "I'd love a wine." she cooed in a breathy voice.

I quickly realized her mistake. "Ah, I don't actually work here." I mumbled.

"I know that. You're the guy in the video."

"Huh?"

"The video. Lenny just said that you're the guy who stokes the fire."

"Well, yeah, but…"

The bartender approached and the redhead caught his eye. "I'd love a wine." she repeated in her sultry voice.

The bartender answered gruffly. "Red or not red?" he asked her.

"Red." she replied, before turning her attention back to me.

"Now, let's talk about stoking fires."

"Huh?" I said, again.

The bartender delivered a glass of red wine onto the stained planks in front of us. The redhead picked up the wine and slowly took a sip, licking her lips as she finished.

"My name's Debbie." she said.

"Huh?" I repeated.

Pleasantries over, she went right in for the kill.

"Fire stoking is super hot." she observed. I was starting to clue into the fact that by "hot", she didn't mean the temperature of the burning logs. "And you do an excellent job of it."

I wanted to say "Oh, thank you so much. I appreciate that you recognized my talent and appreciated my artistic achievement."

Instead, I said "Huh?"

Red continued, and now she had my full attention.

"Women can stoke fires, too, you know."

Another "Huh?" During my next shift at the bookstore, I'm going to steal a thesaurus.

"Oh yes." she said. "A woman knows how to stoke *all kinds of fires and bring on the heat.*"

I don't remember – or at least I won't repeat – much after that, but I woke up in her apartment the next morning as she stood in a bathrobe, brushing out her flaming red hair, post-shower.

She stretched her arms into the air, showing off her magnificent form.

"What a night." she sighed.

Then she slipped out of her bathrobe and into her work clothes for the day. I slid out of her bed and found my clothing by following the trail of hastily shed garments back down the stairs and through the hallway to the front door. She joined me there and leaned in to share a soft kiss before we stepped out into the sunlight of a winter's morning in Los Angeles.

"My first celebrity." she said, before stealing another quick kiss and disappearing into the foot traffic on La Cienega Boulevard.

"Huh!" I said triumphantly as I rubbed my eyes, and began walking towards Burbank.

Now, I knew that Leonard, with my help, had created a holiday favourite. Beginning with that Christmas season, the "Yule Log" video was everywhere and Leonard was rolling in money. I wasn't doing too badly, either. The 10% royalty was a nice supplement to my bookstore salary – the bookstore where I was now general manager. And I knew that, in terms of broadcast licensing and home video sales, we had a hit on our hands.

What I didn't know was that women (and some men) all over America were watching that video and FANTASIZING about the guy in the green flannel shirt. I had told myself that the redhead – what was her name? Oh, right, Debbie – was a one-off. But I soon discovered that my cache as a seasonal celebrity could get me a lot of attention.

December became a long
parade of mistletoe and
strange mattresses.

And it wasn't just the sexual
cornucopia that came my
way. I stopped having to
pay for drinks, I autographed
copies of the VHS tape and
sold photographs of my arm
beside a fire – extra for an autographed one. I quit my job
at the bookstore. I heard later that it burned down.

I even got hired to do "live shows" at clubs, private homes,
and charities. For a live fire-stoking gig, I'd show up, collect
a few hundred dollars (always cash, always in advance),
then wait patiently as the organisers started a fire in a
fireplace. Once the logs had burned for a bit, I'd pick up
the poker, someone would announce me, and I'd walk to
the hearth and shove the logs around until the flames rose
up the chimney. Audiences would applaud, and women
would swoon. It seemed that everybody wanted to be my
friend. Booze was plentiful, and cocaine was ever-present.
For the hero of the "Yule Log" video, nothing made
more sense than getting wrecked nightly in a blinding
snowstorm.

Leonard and I began to communicate exclusively through
our lawyers. I demanded (and got) my name on the cover
of every copy of "Yule Log" sold. Leonard demanded (and
did *not* get) a percentage of my live performance fees.
Because... fuck him.

I stoked fires at the famous Magic Castle, I stoked at Robert Duvall's mansion, I stoked at Hillcrest Country Club. For charity, I stoked at Cedars-Sinai as they raised money at a Tourette's fundraiser - the ailment that causes uncontrollable twitching and verbal outbursts. I stoked at a fundraiser for Multiple Sclerosis (MS), the debilitating disease that can cause a victim to hear the sound of bells ringing in their ears. And I stoked for hand, foot, and mouth disease, a condition where patients' skin blisters up. I wore work gloves for that one and didn't shake any hands.

As the stoking appearances became more frequent, the demands that I made of presenters became more outrageous. I required, and always got, limousine service to and from the gigs. I was provided with a sizeable "green room" where I could rest, eat, drink, change into "the shirt" and then get myself into the character of "fireplace dude" before appearing. The green room was to include a bottle of fine Remy Martin cognac and some high-end snacks. And if, during the job, an attractive woman made eye contact and looked interested, I would brazenly ask someone from the presenting organisation to invite her back to my green room for a nice glass of cognac and some caviar-covered gourmet crisps.

It literally never failed.

And do you know what I've heard over the years? "Oh, I bet you're rugged." "I love a man who can stoke a fire. It's very... primitive." "If you can warm me up, you can have me."

I bedded a couple of television executives who bemoaned my lack of an Emmy. I felt that Leonard had probably held me back.

The live events became more and more extravagant. I would often be paired with classic Christmas movies.

I saw them all, dozens of times. I watched "A Christmas Carol" with Alistair Sim's Scrooge redeemed by the visits of three ghosts. *"Are there no prisons? Are there no work houses?"* I practically memorized "It's a Wonderful Life" with Jimmy Stewart's George Bailey stopped from plunging off a bridge to his death by Clarence, the Angel. *"Look, Daddy! Teacher says every time a bell rings, an angel gets his wings."* And I can tell you every shot and scene of "Miracle on 34th Street" with little Natalie Wood testing her mother's scepticism about Santa Claus. Of all of them, I think it was "Christmas in Connecticut" — about a magazine writer who pretends to be a domestic goddess — that hit the closest to home for me. But such is the fate of any celebrated artist, we all feel like imposters.

However, as the 80s became the 90s, the live gigs mysteriously began to dry up. I blame the new Puritan ethos that was sweeping America fuelled by John DeLorean's cocaine bust, STDs, Jerry Falwell, Ronald Reagan, and the advent of the Bush Presidential dynasty. Suddenly, nobody had the courage to present the ultimate in hedonistic servitude — a man who stoked your fire for you. I don't know for sure that I was ever under surveillance by the FBI, but it makes sense. Had I become political, I could have been a powerful force for societal dissent.

With fewer and fewer outlets for my art, I had to take my act to the streets, to the people. I launched a grassroots campaign. I took to wearing "the shirt" and making random appearances in bars, restaurants, and nightclubs – anywhere people were gathered while the "Yule Log" video was being shown. If nobody recognized my arm, I'd casually mention my starring role in the video and the circus of adulation and alcoholic alteration would begin all over again.

What they don't tell you when you become a celebrity is that time will eventually rob you of your fame, your looks, and, possibly, your talent. As the years passed, each new liaison seemed more desperate than the last and "wear the shirt" was more often the fantasy of the twice-divorced than the angelic nubile searching for some comfort in the bleak mid-winter.

And then, one day in the middle of the 90s, online streaming arrived.

Suddenly, "Yule Log" could be pirated in Singapore, Moscow, and Manchester with no payment to its rights owners (which now included me – I had successfully sued for a 35% interest in the master property, squeezing Leonard down to 65%. Because… fuck him). Within a couple of years, the Internet was awash with pirated copies and foreign knock-offs.

So when it became obvious to me that my life as a celebrity was at an end, usurped by a younger, sexier, CHEAPER arm from Korea with tiny fingers and a little poker, I was devastated. I wandered the streets, inconsolable, until finally, I found myself in a snowstorm, standing on a bridge, overlooking an icy river. And waiting.

Scenes of Jimmy Stewart were flashing through my mind. Where was my Clarence? *"Every time a bell rings, an angel gets his wings."*

A bell rang. I heard it.

I probably have MS.

E.T. Did Not Die For Our Sins

I am not a religious person. And maybe this is why. Sometime in the early 1980s, I began to notice that Christmas tree ornaments were appearing with a distinct pop culture twist.

Now, I grew up in the 70s and 80s with my parents' blown glass ornaments from Germany. Imported German Christmas ornaments were a big deal in the 1950s. I think it was our way of saying "Sorry for kicking your butt in that whole war thing."

Additionally, there were some clear plastic shells with Santas or trees in them, angels, and assorted baubles covered with thin, golden thread and sequins. On the top of the tree, an angel. And spread throughout, that Goddamned tinsel! Strands of silvery plastic that my mother insisted could only be applied by wrapping the end of each strand twice (not once, not three times) clockwise around the tip of every branch of the tree.

I still hate tinsel.

And I am only now realizing that my mother may have had OCD.

Christmas ornaments on my family's tree were traditional, bright, and sparkly. They did not include spaceships, aliens, or supervillains. Sometimes a Garfield would sneak his way into the mix. And there were annual Charlie Brown themed ornaments that became a "thing" in the late 80s, but for the most part, the *Christmas* tree was a haven of *Christmas* decorations. And even Garfield and Charlie Brown were benign. For kids of the 70s, Charlie Brown practically IS Christmas. It's important to note that Charlie Brown never blew up a planet and Garfield never vaporised an intergalactic collections agent.

So what the actual fuck is Darth Vader doing wearing a Santa hat and hanging out on a shelf at the Hallmark store beside Hermey the dentist elf?

Don't get me wrong. I understand that Darth Vader is a fictional character. And I understand that, according to his son, Luke, "there is good in him."

And Luke, let's be honest, has every reason in the Galaxy to be super pissed at his genocidal deadbeat dad. First, there's 19 years of missed soccer games and unpaid child support. But then, I mean, really, Vader's big act in the first (or fourth – I've lost track – whichever one came out in 1977) "Star Wars™" movie is to blow up Luke's sister, Princess Leia's, home planet of Alderaan. Yep, an ENTIRE FUCKING PLANET! Oh, but there's "good in him". Let's hang him on the tree among the tinsel wearing a Santa hat - the ultimate symbol of generosity - to give little Timmy something to aspire to. And we wonder why we're electing mentally defective monsters to govern us?

We don't even acknowledge the BILLIONS of victims of Alderaan (estimated population: over two billion according to some geekfuck website). Nowhere have I seen "glistening chunks of Alderaan" marketed as ornaments. And I haven't seen an Obi-Wan ornament with a pull-string who says "As if millions of voices cried out in terror". Nope, the ornamental glory all goes to the sonofabitch who oversaw construction of the Death Star and then ordered some helmeted flunky to pull the planet blaster lever. Weird.

NOT that I think there should be Alderaan memorial ornaments! In fact, though I may start sounding curmudgeonly, Christmas to me needs to be about goodness and tradition. Whether you buy the magic baby in the manger story as told or not, if you celebrate Christmas, it is, at its essence, a holiday rooted in hope, redemption, and generosity. "Ah ha!" I hear you say "Vader redeems himself at the end of 'Jedi' by tossing the Emperor into a big glowing laser hell pit."

Okay. Yes. But again, murderous maniac on a grand scale. Slaughters a bunch of child Jedi, blows up planets. One act of nepotistic revenge does not really make him into our Lord and Saviour. So piss off. And Picard is a better captain anyway.

Most of you are scratching your heads. Trent in Des Moines is boiling with rage because I mixed together his two favourite sci-fi franchises.

Where was I? "Working through some childhood issues" I hear you say. And you're probably right.

So, I went down a rabbit hole called "Strange Christmas Tree Ornaments". And strange doesn't even BEGIN to describe the things that I've found.

Every cinematic serial killer you can think of has a Christmas tree ornament. Michael Myers (no, not Austin Powers! If you were confused, put this book back on the shelf right now!) has an ornament. Freddy Krueger has an ornament in which he is wrapped in multi-coloured Christmas lights and brandishing a crucifix. Of course, Jason Voorhees ("Friday the 13th") has an ornament. In fact, I found a website called Horrornaments. Horrornaments features not only serial killers, but zombie Santas, undead elves, and a trophy mounted Rudolph head called "Brain Deer".

What. The. Actual. Fuck?

Again, not religious. But pretty clear that Christmas is about magic, and joy, and the laughter of children. Christmas is not about fear, and horror, and the murder of co-eds. That's Hallowe'en you're thinking of. Or possibly summer camp for the promiscuous. It is most decidedly NOT Christmas.

Frosty the Snowman does not wield an axe. He carries a benign broomstick. Santa Claus is not one of the undead, even the New York Sun acknowledged his living existence. And Rudolph does not gore the other eight reindeer to death. Although after all of the name-calling, you could hardly blame him if he snapped. So why has Christmas become twisted and deadly?

I think that we need to blame E.T.

That weird little lizard thing from the 1982 Spielberg movie was the fifth column of creepy Christmas characters who first wormed his way into our hearts, and then our homes. He is often pictured swaddled in a blanket, just like the baby Jesus. Hell, his glowing finger even helps him perform miracles... just like Jesus! And, wait for it, in the movie, he dies AND COMES BACK TO LIFE!!! Just like Jesus.

Except that E.T. is a hideous creature who ultimately coaxed other members of his species to come to Earth in spaceships. I know that the Spielberg movie ends happily, but have you seen "Independence Day" or "Mars Attacks"? That's what aliens are gonna do to us. They're gonna blast our pasty asses. And you know what else? They're going to feel perfectly justified doing it because "Gloop, glob, greep, gloop. G'stoooort." Which is alien speak for "They worship us. We are even on their seasonal plants."

Smart, humans, really smart. Each and every one of you who has indulged their need to see the swaddled Extra Terrestrial on their tree is going to be directly responsible for the obliteration of the human race. Garfield would never do this. Well, maybe on a Monday. Charlie Brown would never do this. Although, God knows, Lucy has provoked him. But aliens? Those bastards are bloodthirsty and you lunatics have elevated them to positions of worship by putting them on your damned CHRISTMAS TREES!!!

So stop it. Darth Vader is not Santa Claus in disguise. Axe murderers should not supplant Wise Men or angels. And E.T. is the point man for an alien invasion. Let Christmas be Christmas. Stop thinking about how and why cute little Anakin turned into Lord Vader. Let go of speculation about eight-year-old Michael Myers dressing up as a clown and murdering his sister. Don't look to the sky hoping that a creature with a glowing booger hook is going to appear.

And, this year, for a change, take a moment to reflect on the origin story of Christmas and the true meaning of the season – shopping for crap! Buying loads and loads of utter crap.

Including this book.

Buy it.

There. Don't you feel better? I know I do.

Merry Christmas.

Hanging Baubles

My family thinks that I'm talented. And so, when my cousin Sharon asked me to help decorate a couple of her outdoor trees because "You do that sort of thing so well", I was not inclined to argue with her.

We agreed upon a mixture. Giant ornaments for one tree with bare branches, and littler ones to "brighten up" a smaller tree.

I went to three different stores to track down oversized Christmas ornaments and at my local Michael's Craft Store, I hit a "2-for-1" sale! Ebenezer Scrooge, that tight-fisted, covetous old sinner, would have been proud of me.

But I digress. What matters here is motive, the warmth of family love, and Sharon's very genuine desire to bring some cheer to her neighbourhood. Now in the second

Christmas of the Covid pandemic, Sharon really wanted her yard to look festive, to "glow". And by the time she'd had lights installed, it really did. And then came the baubles. The extra big ones for one tree, and then a bunch of smaller, really colourful ones for another tree festooned from roots to top in white mini-lights. Even with humility, I have to say that the entire presentation looked really lovely.

It was a clear, chilly December afternoon when I popped by to add a few more decorations and finish up the yard. As I cheerfully hung red, green, and gold ornaments (because you really can't decorate for Christmas if you're not cheerful), Sharon went inside her house to bring me a treat.

When what to my wondering eyes should appear?
Sharon surprised me with half a Tupperware container of shortbread cookies — cookies made EXACTLY from my, from OUR, grandmother's recipe. We called our grandmother "Gran", and though she's been gone almost 40 years, we still remember her fondly.

Christmas at Gran's always included a silver tinsel tree with rotating tricoloured lights under it. It included hard red and green candies. And it included cookies. THOSE cookies. And I am genuinely grateful to Sharon for recreating that sensation for both of us.

Smell and taste are the things that take us back in time — even as far as a happy childhood Christmas memory. It was wonderful. The cookies were just like Gran used to make.

She used rice flour just like Gran used to do.

She baked them to perfection, the edges just a little bit brown, just like Gran used to do.

She brought them outside to me in a Tupperware box with waxed paper lining the bottom. The presentation was just like Gran would have done.

And, as I munched away on the first cookie and hung baubles, Sharon placed the open Tupperware box on the steps of her house so I could snack away as I worked. Just like Gran would have done for me.

But Gran didn't have three young dogs.

Sharon does.

Sharon turned away from the cookies and handed me a shimmering red ornament.

What happened next was like a scene from "Sesame Street" featuring the Cookie Monster.

In an instant, a fine mist of cookie crumbs and dog saliva filled the air over the front steps.

Sharon reached into the maelstrom to try and rescue some cookies, even one cookie.

When she withdrew her hand, I counted her fingers. Some sort of divine intervention had left her with 10.

A very happy dog retreated in one direction with an entire cookie in her mouth. Two other very happy dogs finished the remnants. Sharon, triumphantly, held one cookie in the air!

"Do you want it? None of the dogs touched it!" she exclaimed, proudly.

"Ummm... No, thank you."

I went back to hanging baubles and bringing Christmas cheer to Sharon's front yard.

It's the thought that counts.

Christmas Dildos

Vancouver, on Canada's West Coast, is not, in actual fact, a very "Christmassy" city. It's getting better. But if you've ever been to New York City or London, you know how cities can dress up at Christmas. The Rockefeller Center tree alone is an internationally recognized symbol of the season and part of the special glow that New York puts on at "the most wonderful time of the year".

Enormous baubles, giant trees, and strings upon strings of sparkling lights, some hung over the streets with oversized snowflakes or angels, can turn any city into a glowing Yuletide spectacle. It's good for business, it's good for tourism, and it's good for the mood of the people. Oh sure, there are those who piss and moan about Christmas decorating schemes not being sufficiently inclusive, but to them my advice is "So, add some of your own lights." Besides, no astute business district in the last 50 years ever put out a glowing baby Jesus to frighten non-believers away. Santa, yes. Reindeer, yes. Snowflakes, yes.

But Santa is only terrifying to the naughty class. And we want them to piss off out of town, anyway.

As I said, Vancouver is improving. In December, there are now enormous baubles on Burrard Street. There are lights and glittering snowflakes all along Robson Street. And there is a towering Christmas tree in Robson Square.

Why? Because winter is dark. Winter sucks. Light pushes that darkness away and, above all else, the spirit of the Christmas season is an inclusive, not a competitive, one.

Well, generally.

My friend Tom told me last week that he had read an article that said that the tree at Robson Square is TALLER than the one at Rockefeller Center in NYC.

I cried "Foul!"

Actually, I called him a liar. A dirty, pants-on-fire, liar.

Then I did some research.

Then I wrote him the following email. Actually, I had a couple of drinks, THEN I wrote him the following email:

Dear Tom:

So… further to your <u>wild</u> assertion that the Robson Square tree is TALLER than the Rockefeller Plaza tree, the correct answer is "sometimes".

The Robson Square tree stands 76 feet tall. It is, of course, a sectional artificial tree.

The Rockefeller Square tree, this year, is 72 feet tall. So, yes, in 2018, the NYC tree is, indeed, shorter.

In 2017, the NYC tree was 75 feet tall so, yes, technically shorter, that year.

HOWEVER, in 2016, the year that I was in NYC at Christmastime, the tree was a walloping 94 feet tall!!!! (the record is a full 100 feet in 1999).

Because it is a real tree, a Norway Spruce, the Rockefeller tree varies in height, much like human beings… and puppies.

Meanwhile, the cold, contrived artifice that stands in Vancouver is now, and always will be, 76 feet tall. It can have no hopes, no aspirations; it is a mechanical contrivance. It is the A.I. of Christmas trees and, no matter what dystopian fiction you consume, A.I. never triumphs over biological life.

In more graphic and adult terms, the Vancouver tree is to Christmas trees what dildos are to the male anatomy. Perhaps larger, perhaps nominally more "perfect", but still a cold, plastic substitute that lacks any emotion or genuine performance. Also, dildos never own a house or buy the wine so I am puzzled by the attraction that some women have to them.

But let not my rantings about dildo trees take away from doing some solid research on this subject. The ARTIFICIAL Vancouver tree is enjoying its 12th year of being erected downtown and lit up with power generated by the tears of Canadian schoolchildren who fail their French homework. And each year, it has been a reliable 76 feet tall.

So, I looked up the height of the various Rockefeller trees over the last 12 years (Wikipedia lists them - because, of course they do). Then I added all 12 years of height together and divided that total number (940) by 12. The answer is... (drum roll, please)...

78.3333333333333 feet of magnificent Norway Spruce height!

On average, then, New York City
proudly displays a tree that is TALLER
than Vancouver's Yuletide dildo, so your
newspaper can suck it.

Also, anyone who disagrees with me is a
lying, graceless maggot. That has nothing to
do with the preceding, it just needed to be
said.

That is all.

B.

FROSTY THE SNOWMAN GOES CAMPING

Bitch.

She was a cold, cold bitch.

Was.

Frosty the Snowman, legendary for being the first snowman who had come to life, had not taken well to marriage. At first, he revelled in the experience of having found a mate. The playfulness, the romance, and some unbridled "thumpity thump thump" snowman sex was both a novelty and a pleasure.

Marriage, the idea of marriage, was quite appealing to Frosty who, after all, had only existed as a sentient being for a few months. In the long run, he actually found the entire experience draining.

Mrs. Frosty was, to be accurate, demanding. And when you're a simple-minded snowman, there are only so many career opportunities available to you. And Frosty was just such a simple-minded snowman. Oh, at first, he raked in serious television royalties from licensing deals for a couple of animated specials. Then there were fees from plushies and inflatable lawn decorations. But Frosty's lawyers and manager had a knack for billing massive "expenses and disbursements" against the snowman's diminishing revenue stream. You see, the television specials all carried with them one-time buyouts and the merchandising rights were suddenly, and without prior approval, sold off to a Chinese conglomerate operating out of Beijing. The transfer reduced Frosty's "right of likeness" payments and, once a variety of dubious charges had been deducted, Frosty's cash in hand dwindled to nearly nothing. Even the royalty stream from a biographical song about him had dried up as high profile artists like Barney the Dinosaur and Michael Buble paid next to nothing to record the classic tune.

Although world famous, Frosty was nearly penniless. He was saddled with a dependant wife with no skills and less ambition who spent like one of the real housewives of the North Pole. He became depressed and desperate. Mostly depressed. He was no longer jolly. He was no longer happy. Frosty was an emotional flatline.

He wandered aimlessly down the streets of town. He laughed less and barely played any more. And he certainly didn't dance around. At one point, things got so bad that he sold his corn cob pipe and broomstick to a television memorabilia website. All of the magic of his relationship was gone. Frozen in a loveless marriage, Frosty entirely lost interest in "snowballing" the Mrs.

The showbiz rumour mill being what it is, people speculated that Frosty had put most of his fortune up his button nose. Nothing could have been further from the truth. There was no fortune. Even old, once-loyal friends turned on him. The local traffic cop called him the "S" word.

And so it was on a cold December afternoon, that the impoverished snowman sought out Mr. Jenkins to ask for a job at "Army and Whatnot Camping Supply".

Jenkins took pity on the snowman, but quickly pointed out that if Frosty worked inside the heated store, he would soon be reduced to a pool of water. Frosty sighed, wiped the gathering snow melt off his brow, and headed for the exit. "WAIT!" said Jenkins. "I have an idea."

An hour later, Frosty stood outside the store in the cold December air holding a placard that read "WINTER BARGAINS!"

And dancing.

It was humiliating, but it was work. And Mr. Jenkins paid what he could and offered Frosty an employee discount of 25% on all camping gear.

For three weeks, Frosty danced. TV cameras came, reporters did feature stories, and Frosty experienced a renewed level of fame. And with that fame, came the customers who flocked to the store in numbers Mr. Jenkins hadn't seen in twenty years. "Army and Whatnot Camping Supply" was the only store in the tri-villages area with a living Christmas display. Tents sold, camp stoves sold, sleeping bags sold, and Red Ryder BB guns sold. Frosty was famous again and business was good.

But Frosty was still tired and now he was humiliated. He had been reduced from international superstar to dancing store mascot. And so each day as he danced, he began to scheme. Frosty needed to get himself out of his living hell. Because, just like actual hell, a living hell will ultimately destroy a snowman.

His opportunity presented itself one bleak afternoon when, as an icy drizzle turned into a light snow flurry, Mr. Jenkins motioned to him from inside the store. Frosty cautiously approached the door and opened it just a crack. "Toss me a snowball" said Jenkins. Past the point of caring, Frosty simply scooped a fist-sized piece of snow from his midsection, rolled it up, and tossed it to Mr. Jenkins. Jenkins caught the snowball in one hand. In his other hand, he held a spray can. He looked at Frosty. "Heatproofing!" he said, "From Acme." He sprayed the substance at his outstretched hand and, in an instant, it dried and created a clear heat shield on the snowball. Jenkins placed the snowball on the counter. Then he turned on a nearby space heater and waited.

Five minutes passed. Frosty and Mr. Jenkins stared at the snowball, seemingly untouched by the heat around it. Frosty had to step back from the door to keep from melting. Ten minutes. The snowball was unchanged. "Eureka!" exclaimed Jenkins. "The world's first non-visible, 100% effective heat shield!"

It didn't sell.

Jenkins marked the price down three times, but for the rest of December, no matter how he presented it, the reality became clear. People had no interest in an invisible spray-on heat shield.

Christmas came and went. "Army and Whatnot Camping Supply" held their first Boxing Day Sale in 10 years and the revenue was fantastic. The sale went on for an entire week and during it, Frosty danced like a dervish in the parking lot, welcoming customers and hawking the deals inside the store.

Jenkins was beside himself with gratitude and gave Frosty a month's salary as a bonus and three weeks of vacation. Frosty announced his intention to take the wife winter camping and Mr. Jenkins obliged by handing his favourite snowman a two person tent, on the house!

The next day, Mr. and Mrs. Frosty the Snowman headed for the mountains in an ugly old green station wagon with wood paneling on the sides. "Why couldn't we get an Escalade?" carped Mrs. Frosty. "Because they cost money... dear." replied Frosty through a gritted, icy smile.

Finally, Frosty found a turnoff into the mountains. He wheeled the station wagon up a logging road, then onto a trail of packed snow and ice, and finally stopped at a snow-covered meadow, surrounded by trees. Frosty pulled the tent and camping gear out of the car while Mrs. Frosty sat on her ass in the front seat of the car and used the electric cigarette lighter to trim her nails.

As night fell, the Frostys enjoyed a meal of flavoured ice in the station wagon. Frosty slowly gathered some wood and piled it in front of the tent. Mrs. Frosty finally emerged from the car and sat down in front of the tent. Frosty surveyed the scene with pride. His campsite, the fruit of his hard and humbling labour. His wife, a composite of unique snowflakes all packed together for optimal beauty. And then he struck a match and tossed it into the pile of firewood.

"Are you crazy?!" gasped Mrs. Frosty.

"We'll be fine," said Frosty. "A campfire is all part of the experience. We're out here in the ice and snow, what could go wrong?"

"I guess," said Mrs. Frosty. "It's just that you're a bit of a dimwit and…"

"I work in a camping store. I know what I'm doing."

The fire sparked and crackled as the flames leapt into the night sky. Burning logs turned into glowing embers. The heat increased.

"I don't feel well." said Mrs. Frosty.

"I know." said Frosty, not looking at her. He gently stoked the fire with a long stick.

A few minutes later, Frosty sloshed his way through the crime scene and returned to the station wagon. Nobody would miss her, he reasoned. Come summertime, what was left of her would just mix with rainwater and flow down a gravel-laden creek bed into the ocean. Gone.

For the first time since last winter, Frosty felt liberated. Once he'd returned from the mountains, he peeled the Acme Heat Shield ™ off his body and tossed it into a dumpster. He opened the cleaning supply shed near the back door of Mr. Jenkins's store and grabbed a wooden handle. Then, with a broomstick firmly in his hand, he ran down to the village square.

~ Yuletide Mulled Wine And Roast Beast ~

Although most of the stories in this book are humour-based, I thought it would be worthwhile to include an absolutely unbeatable recipe for a favourite seasonal beverage, mulled wine.

Mulled wine is one of those things that almost everyone has taken a crack at.

Martha Stewart has published her recipe. If you can assemble all of the ingredients without having a stroke, you're a better person than I. Allspice berries. What the actual FUCK are allspice berries?

Who cares?

Actually, I did some research. Allspice berries are from some tropical plant and are meant to taste like a combination of cloves, cinnamon, and nutmeg.

I have an idea. Just put those things into your mulled wine and stop pissing about with a berry that you'll only use once a year, if that.

Here's my recipe. It's super simple. I think that I nicked it from a rock and roll drummer friend of mine. Oh, and it's also really, really good. But don't let Andrew have too much of it (he's a lightweight). And definitely don't try to eat the orange the next morning. You'll feel like you've been kicked by a donkey.

So, take…

1 bottle of cheap red wine (750 ml or who knows in fluid ounces)

¼ cup brandy

2 cups water

½ cup sugar

15 cloves

1 lemon peel

1 cinnamon stick

1 whole orange

First, take the orange and cloves. Stick the cloves into the orange by their stems in a pattern that looks like a happy face. The happy face should roughly look like the paper target that Mel Gibson shoots up in "Lethal Weapon" (the first one, before they got shitty). This is very important. If you don't do this, the mixture will be utterly undrinkable. Now, watch "Lethal Weapon" which is as much of a Christmas movie as "Die Hard". Neither are Christmas movies. I will fight you on this. And I'll have a few glasses of mulled wine in me. Just concede.

Zest the lemon and put the zest into a tea ball. If you don't do this, the zest will float about in the liquid and you'll have to strain each glass of wine as you pour it. Maybe you'll have a strainer, maybe you'll have to steal a pair of your girlfriend's pantyhose to use as a strainer. And then throw them out. And then come up with a lie about why a pair of your girlfriend's pantyhose are missing. It doesn't matter, she's going to dump you in about six months anyway.

Put everything EXCEPT the wine and brandy into a pot. Yep, put the sugar, cinnamon stick, happy orange, tea ball of lemon zest along with the 2 cups of water in a pot. A big pot. Big enough to then take the bottle of wine and ¼ cup of brandy. If the pot is too small, the wine and brandy will spill onto your nice, white stove. And dried red wine is a bugger to clean off white enamel the next morning. Or so I've heard.

Now, bring it to heat. In fact, fuckit, you can even boil this mixture. After 10 minutes of heat, add wine and brandy. Stir gently, do NOT overheat this potion, and once it's filled your home with the most glorious, Christmassy smell imaginable, pour it into Christmas-themed coffee mugs and serve it to your guests.

Now, turn on Christmas music. I recommend the Vince Guaraldi Trio's jazz masterpiece, "A Charlie Brown Christmas".

Or the soundtrack from "Lethal Weapon".

Your call.

New Year's Roast Beast Dinner

PRIME RIB ROAST

3 rib roast – serves 10-12 freeloading bastards.

Apply a simple rub of salt and pepper and, if available, black garlic to the outside of the roast before placing it on a rack in a pan. Line the pan with tinfoil so that you're not scrubbing as the ball drops in New York – or Hawaii.

Preheat the oven to 450 degrees Fahrenheit. Put the roast in for 10 – 15 minutes to brown and seal in the juices.

Turn the oven down to 325 degrees F and allow 3 hours (or set to 350 degrees F and allow 2.5 hours). Watch the meat thermometer to determine the time to take it out.

As soon as the thermometer hits the half-way point in the "rare beef" zone (just under 140 degrees F), remove the meat from the oven.

Let stand for no less than 15 minutes, but no more than 30, so keep your shit together in terms of timing the vegetables and potatoes.

If anyone complains about the rareness of the beef, give them $20 and send them out for a pizza. Lock the front door. Hope it snows.

GRAVY

2 Tbsp drippings

2 Tbsp flour

Stir over heat until thick, cook until brown.

Add remainder of drippings (which won't be all that much from a prime rib roast).

Toss in 2 plus cups of water and add one cube OXO gravy - or a satchel if they aren't making cubes.

Salt and pepper. Easy with the salt! The OXO is kinda salty to begin with.

And (very important) 3 or 4 Tbsp of MULLED WINE (see previous recipe).

Stir until simmering nicely, serve with beef, and await compliments.

Macy's LoveLand

Macy's New York department store was struggling. From American Thanksgiving until Christmas, Macy's churns out more cash than the US mint trying to end the Great Depression.

And the reason for this is simple. Oh, sure it's Christmas and everyone is in a buying frenzy trying to prove their love or at least get a gift that will yield some coveted Yuletide nookie. Sometimes both. But on top of that, Macy's has THE best Santa Claus system in the world: Macy's SantaLand. In SantaLand, you can visit the old boy, have your picture taken, interact with elves, and feast your eyes on a wonderland of magical trees, reindeer, snowflakes, and sparkling toadstools before you, freshly inspired, venture back out into the store and BUY SOME MORE!

But the moment the Christmas season is over, VISA shock sets in and the spending stops entirely. This is where I come in.

I am what is known as a Freelance Retail Fixer (FRF in the biz). I go from store to store suggesting promotions, deals, and events to kickstart the revenue-challenged. And I'm damned good at what I do. FOURTH generation FRF! My great grandfather in Streatham, England invented the "2 for 1" sale, my grandfather created Bargain Tuesdays, and my father designed and built the first shopping buggy.

So there I was in January in the middle of a very swanky lounge in a very swanky hotel in the middle of 44th Street about to down a very swanky drink in a very swanky glass when my cell phone rang. It was J. Egleston Brahms, the General Manager of Macy's Worldwide. And when Mr. Brahms calls, you answer.

"Good afternoon, sir..." I began. He cut me off. He sounded desperate. "Allman, we're in trouble! Projections have us down 47% over last Q" ("Quarter" for those who don't know).

I tried my best to reassure him.

"Sir, January is always a slug after Q4."

"I KNOW!" he howled, expressing the only emotion that I'd heard him express in 30 years.

"But a 28% drop was our record low, and this is a full 19 points down from that! We're doomed! If we can't pull this quarter up, we'll have to... (he paused, contemplating the unthinkable, then he whispered, nearly hysterical) ***sell 34th Street.***

"Sweet Baby Jesus!" I thought. "Sell 34th Street in New York City? THE flagship store? THE largest retail store in America? THE store that starred in 'Miracle on 34th Street'?"

"NOT ON MY WATCH!!!" I barked boldly at him.

"Can you meet me?" he whispered, desperate, imploringly. "But not at the store."

"How about Sardi's?" I asked. I love their martinis.

"NO WAY!" he yelped. "Full of culture vultures! Nowhere that people will see us and talk."

I wracked my brain. An FRF is like a Navy SEAL. We operate anywhere and never get to know one place too well. What did I know from New York?

"I know!" he said. "The 2nd Avenue Deli down on 27th Street. Lower East Side. *Your people* love it there."

"*My people*? What the... I'm not..." But he cut me off again.

"Meet me there at eleven o'clock tonight. Come alone," he said, ominously.

"Yes, sir," I said and hung up. Come alone? Well I guess that meant wearing a wire was out. And who was I going to bring? "Hi, Sheila, we met at the Rainbow Room last week. Wanna join me at a business meeting in a deli tonight at eleven? No? Oh… your hair, huh? Okay, maybe another time… Oh. You're leaving town. Forever. Well, my tough luck."

I threw back my very swanky cocktail in the very swanky glass and decided that I should look ominous. So I popped across the street into my hotel to fetch my long, dark overcoat and my deep blue fedora befitting the clandestine nature of my meeting. Common sense and a sharp collision with the wall of my hotel room encouraged me to leave my sunglasses behind for the night. I waited in the room until darkness fell and then took the service elevator down to the kitchen and loading bay. I slipped past a gaggle of wide-eyed Mexican kitchen staff and vanished into the parking garage.

Ten minutes later, I was pacing West 34th Street in front of Macy's, staring at windows that, just a few weeks earlier, had been resplendent with reindeer, and elves, and a seasonal seduction to see Santa… and SPEND.

Now, the windows had all the personality of a Baptist minister with a loaf of Wonderbread and a jar of mayonnaise. Mannequins stood wearing the latest fashion and maybe I was projecting, but I saw hopelessness in their eyes. One mannequin in particular seemed to be saying "You're not going to buy *this*, are you?."

No.

I stood on West 34th Street for almost three hours imagining different possibilities. Winter Wardrobe! The Lion, the Witch, and the Winter Wardrobe! YES! Take a beloved children's tale and turn it into a merchandising campaign! Then I looked online at the most recent book sales figures for the C.S. Lewis classic. That woke me up. Turns out that the Tales of Narnia hold no more place in the modern imagination than Borax.

You had to look up "Borax", right?

See my point?

Finally, it was time to go and meet Mr. Brahms. Just as I turned away from the store window, I caught a glimpse of the Empire State Building, patriotically lit with red, white, and blue. Red. Red. Red hearts. VALENTINE'S DAY!

I ran to the 2nd Avenue Deli.

As I burst through the door, Mr. Brahms had pushed his way through the counter crowd and was trying to order a sandwich.

"TAKEOUT ONLY!" barked the owner, although his sign clearly said that he closed at 11:30, not 11.

Brahms turned to me as if to say "You speak to him, he's one of *your people*." I merely shrugged and ordered a pastrami sandwich to go. "We'll find somewhere," I reassured Mr. Brahms. He opened his mouth to speak. I didn't have the heart to tell him that I'm not Jewish, so I made a production of coughing into the bend of my elbow. The other customers shuffled uncomfortably away from me.

We strode out into the cool New York night air and made our way a few blocks north and east to St. Vartan Park.

Under cover of darkness, we found a bench and opened our sandwiches.

"Please tell me you've got something for me," pleaded Brahms.

"I do," I said, hungrily chewing off a massive bite of delicious, grease and mustard coated pastrami.

"What?! What is it?!" he begged.

"Mwphees Lfnund!" I replied, chewing.

"WHAT?!" he practically shrieked. I held up my hand, the universal sign for "let me chew". Brahms waited impatiently until I swallowed my sandwich bite and took a giant gulp of my Manischewitz concord grape juice.

I swallowed again, washing down morsels of pastrami.

"Macy's LoveLand!" I announced, proudly.

Brahms looked at me, blankly. I went into "pitch mode".

"It's like SantaLand, only for lovers. Your windows will be a mix of Valentine's fashion, Valentine's cards, Valentine's candy, and SEX! Think of high end suits and gowns! Think of Georgia O'Keeffe art cards! Think of repurposing Mrs. Claus's Candy Factory to make chocolate hearts! And think of revealing red lingerie on LIVE models!"

"I like it!" yelped Brahms.

"There's more!" I enthused. "Think of redressing all those animatronic elves as little Cupids with little bows and arrows shooting cards across 34th Street! Your windows will be the talk of the town just like at Christmastime.”

“In fact,” I continued, totally on a roll now, “forget about the animatronics, let’s get ACTUAL CHILDREN to be cherubim!”

“The what?” asked Brahms, confused.

“CUPID!” I yelled with passion and enthusiasm! “Let’s get real children to play Cupid! It’ll be magical.”

Brahms had clearly bought into the program. “I’m in. What will the windows cost?”

“50 grand each!”

“There’s SIX of them!”

“You wanna make money or be remembered as the captain of a sinking ship?”

“I wanna make money!”

“Then we have to do this. Macy’s LoveLand will become an international legend!”

Brahms chewed his sandwich thoroughly.

“How do *you people* not die of heart attacks in your 20s?”

“I’m not...”

But he was calculating and he was vulnerable. It was the wrong time to pick an argument.

“Chosen people, nu?” I said disingenuously.

Brahms nodded knowingly.

"Okay." he said after a long pause. "I'll do it!"

We shook hands and I ignored the drip of sandwich grease that he spread across my palm as we touched.

The next morning, I went to work. I called the best theatre designers in New York. I called the artists who brought sets to life for "Hamilton", for "42nd Street", for "West Side Story", for "The Lion King", for "Wicked", and for "Jersey Boys". "I got 50 grand for you. Give me LOVELAND!" I barked imperiously into the phone. "And email me scanned sketches by Friday."

I guarantee you that not one of them knew who I was. But they knew Macy's. More importantly, they knew how to get paid in advance.

Friday arrived and I signed off on all the submissions. Did they match my vision? That would presume that I had a vision. They all looked frighteningly expensive and given my fee and proposed budget, they needed to look frighteningly expensive. My next call was to Backstage, the agency that represents child actors in New York.

I got a lovely agent on the phone named Barbara. She was very personable and professional. I was in full alpha male mode and so when she asked about my specific project, I blurted out "I need a bunch of scantily clad young children to work on 7th Avenue..."

Barbara hung up.

I reconsidered my approach and called Barbara back. She was, again, professional if a little less warm this time. But we finally made a personal connection. I explained what I did as an FRF, and she explained that her husband, brother, and father were all members of New York's finest… the police department.

When I finally outlined the project, Barbara assured me that she could fulfill all my casting needs. I may have glossed over the fact that we'd be arming the children with bows and arrows.

My next call was to Official Models NY who, their web presence suggested, specialized in underwear models. After a brief chat with one of their reps (it's "biz" talk for representatives"), I was convinced to try a more "cost-conscious" agency that might prove to be less, erm, "discerning".

10 phone calls later, I landed on Satan's Seduction Syracuse, an agency that operated outside of the city, but that carried strong recommendations. After a bit of back and forth, Mel, their agent, agreed to send "twenny o' my best broads" to model select pieces of Macy's underwear in the various windows. I then turned my attention to finding a matching number of men to "work" the various displays in selected skivvies. Steve Models turned out to be the finest male modelling agency in NYC (according to the Steve website) and Claire was clearly happy to make Macy's into a client. She assured me that she would send out 20 pieces of "irresistible beefcake"; men who, while mostly new to modelling, were driven, committed

denizens of the service industry, and "extremely high energy".

I should have considered what "extremely high energy" might mean.

But we were steaming ahead to February 1st, our announced, and committed to, opening day! Brahms and I had selected the 1st in order to capture TWO weekends prior to Valentine's Day and to give us a good run of sales. Ads were designed, press releases sent, feature pieces on New York One were even aired with various designers slamming doors on the camera crew to "create mystery". I'm a big fan of creating mystery when you don't actually have a finished product to show off.

Finally, the big day was upon us. The set designers responsible for each window had also brought along members of the costume and makeup departments to provide "finishing touches" to the live models that would blend with the scenic themes.

On 34th Street, it seemed as if all of New York had come out to see the "big reveal". I moved through the crowd, beaming with anticipation and pride at what I'd accomplished. Mr. Brahms met me on the street, his eyes positively shining with expectation of the record profits clearly heading his way. "Each one of these people is going to drop almost a grand inside Macy's!" he enthused. I wasn't sure where he got his numbers from, but I was concerned by the state of some of the prospective customers' clothing. There were a lot of threadbare suit jackets, worn out sneakers, sweatpants, and sports team wear from New Jersey.

"Holy shit!" I thought to myself. "This is the bridge and tunnel crowd!"

Perhaps running a full page in the Hudson County News instead of the New York Times had been an error. But my palpitations slowed as I saw an influx of city dwellers descending on us from the 33rd Street Station. Serious money was upon us and if they were charmed, we would reap the benefits.

I glanced at my watch. 11:57. In three minutes, my stage manager buddy Dave would coordinate the opening of the first-ever Macy's LoveLand. The windows were done and guaranteed to be magical. Sound systems over the sidewalk would blast the best show tunes from each vignette to the adoring ears of the crowd.

Meanwhile, inside the store, the area normally assigned to SantaLand had been converted to a faux hedge maze dotted with classical statues and impressionist paintings by some of the masters. There were Van Goghs, Monets, Degas, and throughout, a high-end speaker system pumped out the finest of classical tunes, romantic poetry, and love songs from the 20th Century American Songbook. It was through here that 100 winged, cherubic Cupids would dash playfully, giggling, their little togas billowing behind them as they bestowed love upon all who entered. I smiled, my heart full of pride at the sheer magnitude of this retail offering.

11:58. "Fly me to the moon and let me play among the stars…" lilted through LoveLand. A woman in a black leather bra with red crotchless panties walked past me. She had green skin.

"Uh… what?" I started. She crammed a witch's hat onto her head. "I'm from Oz!" she proclaimed and stumbled a little as she entered the door to a window marked "Wicked".

Four musclebound Italian-looking men were hacking their way through "Sherry Baby" in tuxedos. They entered the "Jersey Boys" section, sniffling between verses. New York's famous winter cold, I guessed.

11:59… I saw the woman in charge of "The Lion King" window nursing four even scratches on her arm. Intrigued as I was, I wanted to be out on the sidewalk for zero hour.

And, precisely at noon, our crew pulled down the paper window covers and the six-window romantic pastiche came to life!

Mr. Brahms and I stood together on the sidewalk taking in the impact of our creative labours.

The "Hamilton" window was first. In front of a brick and timber wall, thick with graffiti, three men in Revolutionary war jackets and Speedo bathing suits coloured, respectively, red, white, and blue, were frenetically throwing various gang hand signs out to the City. Behind them, three women wearing undergarments definitely NOT purchased at Macy's were waving beer steins and grinding seductively to a pulsing techno beat.

To their credit, they were, at least, co-ordinated in their movements.

In the "42nd Street" display, a gigantic mirror was angled to provide a stunning view to the audience; a view that centred on three men in spats and underwear, carrying shiny canes, strutting over top of three leggy and virtually naked dancers lying on their backs and kicking their legs as if in a synchronized swimming contest.

The "Wicked" vignette featured the green-skinned woman I had seen earlier now straddling a vintage witch's broom while the Good Witch "Glinda" looked on in pink suspenders, panties, and a bra. "Dorothy's" gingham skirt was hiked up and her toy plushie "Toto" was doing duty as a cover up of her most intimate region. The men in that window were dressed in Fez caps, vests, and tighty whitey underwear, suspended from the ceiling as "Flying Monkeys". Periodically, the green-skinned woman would shriek out "FLY MY PRETTIES!" and the three men would go into paroxysms of flight – flapping their arms, snarling at the crowd outside, and vigorously wiping their noses.

The "Jersey Boys" window had attracted most of the Jersey crowd. Men and women in New Jersey Devils, New York Jets, and New York Giants t-shirts and hats were screaming "WOO!" at full volume. The set was the hardscrabble industrial New Jersey skyline of the 50s. Suddenly, the four tuxedos worn by the Italian-looking guys tore away to reveal black satin briefs. Behind the "Four Seasons", four women in housewife attire were pulling on cigarettes and sucking on lipstick tubes. In a flash, at the peak note of

"Big Girls Don't Cry", the pretty dresses dropped and the four housewives, clad only in high heels, thong underwear, and tight, white "Macy's" t-shirts, gyrated as they climbed a series of four water towers before pulling a chain at the top and dousing themselves with actual water. It was like "Flashdance"… for adults. Depraved adults.

In "Westside Story", where the "set" was a chain link fence wrapped around a brick façade, two Puerto Rican men were actually beating the shit out of two white men while four bikini-clad women pretended to care. There was blood. Real blood. I cringed and hoped that there were no real switchblades.

And then, the "piece de resistance," the window dedicated to "The Lion King". A masterful recreation of the Serengeti complete with the rock upon which the infant lion cub is hoisted for all to see. A man lifted an ACTUAL lion cub into the air! The crowd on the sidewalk swooned. The lion cub looked singularly unimpressed and I noticed a few scratch and bite marks on the man. But the music swelled and the offering moment brought the colourfully and thinly clad "villagers" out to worship the new King of the Jungle. Four muscley men and four buxom dancer beauties raised their eyes, faces, and arms towards the uplifted Simba.

And every single model was in blackface.

I considered suicide.

I felt Mr. Brahms clutch my arm with the intensity of an electrocution victim. Putting on a brave face, I turned, smiled broadly, and enthused "That'll make the papers! Let's see what's inside."

I was convinced that the flights of angels inside the store would lift the audience up and carry them away from the spectacle of the windows on 34th Street. As Brahms and I headed for the doors, we heard the first rock hit "The Lion King" window.

Inside, the few customers who had drifted past the front door were treated to an experience like no other. The maze and the music were transformative. The spoken love poems, and the pieces of fine art, took you to another place altogether. And then the minders released their pantheon of toga and sandal-clad Cupids to dart ethereally about the heartfelt wonderland where they would embody and spread romance. I was at ease once more as I saw my initial vision realized.

When I first conceived of Macy's LoveLand, THIS was the image that I'd seen in my mind. I had seen the wonder of childhood floating through the retail space, blessing each happy couple with thoughts and wishes of love. I had thought about the joy of children. I had thought about the magic of children. I had thought about the innocence of children.

I had not considered the
reality of children.

Children with bows and
arrows.

Although the arrows were
tipped with red velvet
hearts, a wooden shaft flying
through the air propelled by
a pulled bowstring can still blind a person. Or two. Closer
to 30 when I last reviewed the lawsuits.

Arrows filled the sky over Macy's LoveLand. Brahms
and I hit the deck as 100 screaming, bow-shooting,
sugar-jacked children went absolutely wild throughout
the store. Display cases toppled and arrows hit people,
walls, and clothing with sickening "thunks". Staff cowered
and customers fled in droves, never to return. Macy's
Valentine extravaganza had turned into a re-enactment of
the battle of Agincourt where the English longbow bested
the French infantry. And once again, the French infantry
realized that they were beaten and went into a full retreat,
taking with them their limitless VISA cards.

So, there's the story. Mr. Brahms was summarily dismissed
the next morning after members of the Board of Directors
were allowed past the detectives of the NYPD and the fire
and flood restoration specialists.

The last I heard, Brahms was running a convenience store in Des Moines and recovering from injuries sustained in a third robbery of that location.

As for me, well, my break's over.

Thanks for reading this. I have to be back on the cash register in a moment.

It's only $10 an hour, but baby, I'm still in retail!

My Baby's Going To Jail For Christmas

A criminal courtroom is a horrible place. Nobody is in criminal court because they're happy. Someone will have been victimized. There will likely be witnesses. There will always be an accused. And, though we're not really supposed to say it, they will generally have "done it".

Oh, I know, I know. Your third cousin's best friend's son's classmate was falsely accused of stealing a car in Etobicoke, Ontario. Take my word on this: the little shit did it.

This doesn't mean that wrongful accusations and convictions don't happen. Of course they do. But they are really rare. Tragic when they occur (and they occur too often in the atmosphere of cultural conflicts), but rare.

Seriously, the little shit in Etobicoke stole the car. He's lucky he got away with it. Don't lend him your car keys.

When you spend your day surrounded by human misery, you develop a dark sense of humour. It becomes your go-to emotional and psychological defense. The judges, lawyers, bailiffs, and court staff deal with an onslaught of professional upset by making jokes. About everyone. Don't for a moment believe that the "gallows humour" is reserved exclusively for the bad guys. If you're in one of those courtrooms, after hours, in the lounge, you're getting metaphorically hanged. Particularly if you wore ugly shoes.

Darlene is a lawyer, a Crown Prosecutor. Her job is to put bad people behind bars. And she is exceptional at her job.

In the U.S.A., a Crown Prosecutor would be a "District Attorney". But here in Canada, we call them Crown Prosecutors and we don't elect them so there's no competition to see who has had the most people killed in the electric chair.

Come to think of it, we don't have electric chairs in Canada, either. Or capital punishment.

But piss off one of our goalies and you'll get a hockey skate to the head.

Darlene lives in the far north of Canada. She practices law in a remote, frozen wasteland where there are only three types of people: lawyers, criminals, and Darlene's parents. Come to think of it, there must be some cops too – mostly there so that Darlene's parents don't turn to a life of crime.

I've known Darlene for almost 20 years. We met when she was a student and I was already practising an entirely different field of law. She became a Crown Prosecutor and before we could order a second Starbuck's coffee, she had moved north. I have never been to where Darlene lives. We talk every few weeks on the phone. For almost 20 years, there have been regular and often entertaining emails. But she's described the place where she lives and I am a former history student. Her description sounds suspiciously like the kind of terrain where Napoleon lost most of his army. All this to say: "If you're reading this Darlene, love you, but fuck off, I'm not coming to visit."

Where was I? Oh, right, Darlene and I stay in touch. And, while she is very careful to never offer up identifying information, she sometimes lets me know about an especially funny moment in her professional life. And, in the winter of 2003, one such moment happened.

"B?" said the voice on the phone. We use each other's first initials as our nicknames. Comes from my habit of signing off emails with a simple "B" because I'm too lazy to put my name in full.

"D!" I exclaimed. "What's happening?"

"I have a challenge for you." she said.

"Go on." I replied.

"Well, you write lyrics, right?"

"I've been known to, yes."

"Here's something one of my colleagues said today. A dude got sentenced to six months and his girlfriend broke down sobbing in court.

My colleague turned to me and said, "Aw, my baby's going to jail for Christmas."

We both laughed.

"Turn it into a song for me."

"What?"

"It's a great chorus."

"It really is. Okay, let me see what I can do."

Those who know me know that simply writing a lyric from a hook phrase like "My Baby's Going to Jail for Christmas" is a challenge that I'll not only accept, but will revel in. Those who really know me also know that I'm not likely to stop at a written lyric. And so, about three weeks later, Darlene opened a padded envelope postmarked from my address in Vancouver. Inside it was a CD. I had written the lyric and recruited some musical friends to compose a tune, produce, and record the song. And here it is, competing for airtime with "Silent Night"…

My Baby's Going to Jail for Christmas

(prelude)
Well, you went out one night in October,
With a gun, and an old pair of my stockings.
And you held up a convenience store.
Then the po-lice came a knocking.

(chorus)
We'll be wassailing in the snow,
Hanging 'neath, the mistletoe,
'Cuz my baby's going to jail for Christmas.
We'll be drinkin' all night long.
Singing all those Christmas songs.
And we're happy that he won't be with us.

(verse)
Did you think, when you went inside
Who would keep you warm on Christmas
Eve?
When you feel cold feet in your bunk at
night.
Baby, you know it's your cellmate Steve.

(chorus)
We'll be wassailing in the snow,
Hanging 'neath, the mistletoe,
'Cuz my baby's going to jail for Christmas.
We'll be drinkin' all night long.
Singing all those Christmas songs.

And we're happy that he won't be with us.

(verse)
Ever think that you'd ask old Santy Claus,
For a prison tattoo and a great big carton of
smokes?
Well your brother dropped by and he told me
to ask.
Honey, what's it like when you drop the
soap?

(chorus)
We'll be wassailing in the snow,
Hanging 'neath, the mistletoe,
'Cuz my baby's going to jail for Christmas.
We'll be drinkin' all night long.
Singing all those Christmas songs.
And we're happy that he won't be with us.

(spoken)
Dear baby, Merry Christmas from jail. I've
been punching out license plates, and waitin'
on your mail.
And if you want that conjugal trailer to be a
rockin',
Could you put a shiv, in my stockin'?

(chorus)
We'll be wassailing in the snow,
Hanging 'neath, the mistletoe,
'Cuz my baby's going to jail for Christmas.
We'll be drinkin' all night long.

Singing all those Christmas songs.
And we're happy that he won't be with us.

(spoken)
Uhhhh... wait a minute, what's "wassailing"?
And why is my brother there?
More often than not, there's room for one
more at the turkey table in here.
They've locked me so far away, they're gonna
have to feed me my Christmas dinner with a
slingshot.
Next year, when I get out, I swear.

I'm gonna ruin Christmas.

A few years later, we shot a video for it and let it fly on
YouTube. Over 3,000 views later, well, enjoy it. Even the
uncomfortable bits! Darlene watches it every year.

HEAR THE SONG - SEE THE VIDEO!

FROSTY THE COV-MAN

It started with a runny nose.

No big deal for a snowman. As the temperature goes up and down, their bodies change. And some extra rays of sun practically guaranteed that a few drops of water would run along Frosty's normally frozen face.

But it wasn't sunny. And now the carrot that served as his nose was dripping.

Frosty shrugged it off. "It's just a cold" said the dim-witted snowman.

But it wasn't. When his symptoms persisted for over a week, one of the local children suggested that he should go and get tested.

"Tested?" said Frosty, confused. "Like for spelling in school? For what?"

Frosty was, bluntly, retarded.

"FOR COVID!" snapped little Suzy who had lived nearly half of her five years dealing with nonstop daily stress and anxiety from the Covid-19 pandemic. The pandemic, with its accompanying collection of blathering health officers, epidemiologists, scientists, and conspiracy cranks, had occupied an insufferable amount of bandwidth on the nightly news and around the family dinner table. And now, it seemed possible that little Suzy's best friend, Frosty the Snowman, might just have it.

"Can snowmen even get Covid?" asked Frosty aloud.

"SnowPEOPLE!" shrieked Suzie, because even at age five, she was very woke.

"Sorry." said Frosty, "I didn't mean to upset you. But can snowpeople get Covid?"

"I don't know" blubbered Suzie, "but you should get checked anyway."

And so, Frosty picked up his broomstick and began to make his way down the streets of town to the testing centre. As he walked, men and women pulled their children out of his way.

"Wear a mask, moron!" shouted one man. So Frosty pulled a face mask out from under his hat and wrapped it around his mouth and over his carrot nose.

"Nice mask you fukkin' commie sheep!" yelled another man from a pickup truck.

Frosty didn't know what any of that meant so he just continued on his way. When he got to the testing center, the beleaguered nurse who administered tests just looked at him.

"Have you been vaccinated?" she asked with all the enthusiasm of a patient in a dentist's chair.

"No, I'm a snowman." replied Frosty.

"Oh, great." said the nurse, "One of you."

"Beg pardon?" said Frosty, trying to decide if he should be offended.

"What are your symptoms?" she droned.

"My nose is runny." said Frosty.

"Sore throat or headache?" asked the nurse, looking distractedly at her cuticles.

"I don't think so." said Frosty. "My head and throat are made of snow and they feel just fine."

"Temperature?" inquired the nurse, licking her thumb and trying to remove some dried jam from her sweater sleeve.

"If I had a temperature, I'd melt away!" exclaimed Frosty.

"Here's a home test kit. Go away." said the nurse, obviously indifferent to Frosty's health situation.

Frosty took the kit with him and walked out the door. Back in Suzy's yard, he opened the kit and tried to read the instructions. None of it made any sense to him. Snowpeople aren't great at reading, to begin with, and the instructions in the test kit used a lot of really big words. Suzy joined him in the yard and scoured the directions for herself.

"It's very ableist and Eurocentric!" proclaimed Suzy, proving once again that she really was annoyingly woke.

Frosty scratched his head, puzzled, but the two of them persevered and eventually collected a swab sample from the moisture on Frosty's carrot nose. Once they were done, they dripped the sample onto the testing device and waited. Suzy looked at the device after 15 minutes. Her face fell a little.

"It's positive." she said, not hiding her disappointment.

"I'll be fine!" effused Frosty. "What could possibly happen to a snowman?"

Suzy was less convinced, but didn't want to disempower her differently-abled friend by challenging his intellect or comprehension. And so she gave the snowman a gentle wave goodnight and wandered off to bed.

When Suzy came downstairs in the morning, she looked out through her front window and was horrified to see Frosty the Snowman lying face down on the front lawn. Frantically pulling on her boots and her winter coat, Suzy dashed to the snowman's side.

"FROSTY! What's wrong?" she cried out.

"Can't... breathe..." gasped the snowman from under his crumpled top hat.

"OH NO! Stay there, I'm going to get you help!" exclaimed Suzy, as she raced inside and dialled 9-1-1.

"Fire, police, or ambulance?" answered a dispatcher who sounded just as excited about life as the nurse in the testing centre.

"AMBULANCE!" cried Suzy. "My best friend is dying from Covid!"

"Is your best friend male or female?"

"Gender fluid!" sniped Suzy, eager to make this a teachable moment.

"Very well." said the dispatcher. "And how old are... they?"

"I don't really know. But they're down on the ground outside my house and they can't breathe."

After gathering Suzy's information, the dispatcher assured her that someone would be "right over".

When the ambulance slid to a stop in front of Suzy's house, two very intense paramedics got out and rushed over towards the little girl.

"I'm Felicia. Where's your friend?" asked one paramedic who appeared to be a woman, but Suzy knew better than to assign a gender role on a first meeting.

"He's, she's, they're over there!" she said, pointing to the fallen Frosty.

The two paramedics stopped in their tracks.

"Ummm... that's a snowman." said the paramedic, who presented as a man.

"Person!" sniped Suzy, wanting to make sure that this was another teachable moment.

"Snow... people can't be in medical distress." said the first paramedic, who still presented as a woman.

"But they is!" Suzy sobbed.

"Are." corrected the second paramedic, who continued to present as a man, but he said it under his breath so as not to drag the conversation in a new and utterly useless direction.

The first paramedic knelt down beside Frosty and spoke.

"Ummmm... how are you feeling today?"

To her shock, Frosty replied, short-winded.

"Not... not good. I can't breathe."

"Jesus, Phil!" said the paramedic to her partner. "He's alive and in distress."

Phil stared at Frosty for a moment, then he sprang into action.

"Felicia, get the O2 kit!" he snapped as he charged to the ambulance and pulled a large, plastic case out from the back. Felicia opened the side door of the ambulance and, in record time, had a plastic oxygen mask attached to

Frosty's face. She opened the valve on the oxygen tank. A gentle hiss arose from Frosty and he seemed to relax.

"Is that better, sir?" asked Felicia. Suzy opened her mouth to object to the gender stereotyping, but Phil's glare made her think better of it.

"Just let us work." said Phil.

The paramedics examined Frosty. Felicia turned her attention to Suzy. "Can you tell me anything important about his, its, their medical history?" she asked.

Suzy nodded. "He tested positive for Covid yesterday." she whimpered, becoming slightly less annoying.

The two paramedics looked at one another. It was Phil who finally said what needed to be said.

"You're telling me that a snow... man received a positive test for the Coronavirus?"

Suzy nodded.

Felicia and Phil stared at each other for a long moment. Could you cut the romantic tension in the air with a knife? Probably not. But at that moment, the two were eternally bonded by a shared experience of the absurd. After the moment for their unrealized kiss had passed, Phil strapped a blood pressure cuff on Frosty's arm.

"No pressure!" he called.

Felicia moved her stethoscope frantically around the snowman's chest.

"No pulse!" she yelped.

"We're losing him!" cried Phil.

"Noooooo! Frosty!" shrieked Suzy.

"Paddles!" barked Felicia.

"On it!" shouted Phil.

"Frosty!" sobbed Suzy.

Phil opened the large plastic case and turned on the defibrillator machine. It whirred to life and he grabbed the plastic handles of the metal paddles and placed them in the textbook positions on Frosty's chest.

"Clear!" yelled Phil.

"Clear!" replied Felicia as she leaned back from the patient and held Suzy in her arms.

Phil pressed the red switch on the positive paddle and for 0.001 of a second, 3,000 volts of electricity surged through Frosty's torso.

KA-POOFLE!!!!

A cloud of steam exploded from the lawn as Frosty's eyes of coal shot off in two different directions, his magical hat sailed out into the roadway, and his carrot nose, now soft-boiled, flew up and struck

Suzy's forehead where it stuck for a moment before sliding off.

The two paramedics stared in shocked silence at the scene in front of them. Only a small pool of water remained where their patient had been just moments before. Suzy wept, heartbroken. Felicia and Phil packed away their equipment professionally and without a word. Just before they climbed into the ambulance, Felicia turned to Suzy and said "I'm sorry for your loss." Suzy nodded mutely. The paramedics hopped into the vehicle and Phil put it into gear.

They drove slowly down the street and rounded the corner, well out of sight of Suzy, before they began to laugh.

Aunt Louise, The Christmas Whore

Aunt Louise, **my** Aunt Louise, was always a little "off" as my mother used to say. "She means well" as my father used to say. Which was his code for "bless her heart", which was polite code for "moonbat crazy" and "as useless as lips on a chicken".

But it was Aunt Louise who taught me about art. Specifically, she taught me the dangers of art. You see, Aunt Louise took art very seriously. Whether it was a painting, a play at the theatre, a movie, or a song on the radio, Aunt Louise was so much more than an audience member. Aunt Louise was a participant. She could tell you in five or 10 thousand words how any given work was speaking directly **to** her.

Aunt Louise went to see the musical "Cats". And Aunt Louise promptly went to the nearest shelter and "rescued" a dozen or more cats that she brought home and named after the various characters in the musical. There was Mr. Mistoffelees, and, erm, um, I don't know. There were a bunch of cats. I don't remember most of their names. But I do remember the look of relief that would appear on my Uncle Albert's face whenever a cat would run away, never to be seen again.

Even as a cat, I think there can be too much love. And unrealistic expectations that you'll miraculously "mew" in tune to "Memory". Having dished out disappointment for several months on the latter count, most of Aunt Louise's ensemble of cats chose to take parts in touring productions. At least that's what we told Aunt Louise. And it really seemed to make sense.

To her.

And, of course, Aunt Louise went to the movies. Often. Her long-suffering husband, Albert, endured numerous cinematic obsessions. Aunt Louise saw "Casablanca" and, for two entire months, drank nothing but French 75s. She saw "Some Like it Hot" and it was a summer of classic Manhattan cocktails. Then some idiot (my older brother) showed her "The Blues Brothers" on VHS home video and suddenly it was the Orange Whip. John Candy's cop character orders a round of these vile concoctions. But if it was good enough for Uncle Buck, it was good enough for Aunt Louise. At the tender age of 14, I even got to try an Orange Whip. One Orange Whip. Two Orange Whips. Three Orange Whips. Then a stream of orange vomit like I've never seen in my life. 40 years later, I can't even see the colour orange without quietly gagging.

On a trip to France for "cultural enrichment", Aunt Louise managed to drag Uncle Albert into the Louvre to see the Mona Lisa. I suspect that Albert wanted nothing to do with France to begin with, but finding himself there, wanted to see the observation deck of the Eiffel Tower, not some museum. And he probably particularly did not want to visit that museum and spend an HOUR of his life waiting while his dippy wife stared at the Mona Lisa. For the next six months, at all times, Aunt Louise wore an enigmatic smile meant to befuddle the beholder. It wasn't until, at Great Aunt Pamela's memorial, someone asked Louise if she'd been checked for signs of Bell's Palsy that she finally let the Mona Lisa smile leave her face.

And then there was that time that Aunt Louise saw the painting "American Gothic" and made my uncle Albert wear granny glasses and carry a pitchfork any time they were going to a family function where there could be a photographer.

Uncle Albert left soon after that.

Aunt Louise was devastated. She grieved the ending of her marriage the same way she lived her life: she faced her problems head on and scampered deep into a world of art-fuelled fantasy. She made a dress out of curtains in an homage to either the "Sound of Music" or "Gone With the Wind". I have no idea which. She did keep screaming "As God is my witness, I'll never be hungry again!", so I guess it was "Gone With the Wind." Thankfully, we didn't live in Atlanta so she didn't get a chance to burn our home town to the ground. I'm pretty certain she'd have tried if we HAD lived in Atlanta. So, one more good reason to not be living in Atlanta – my Aunt Louise and a pack of matches. Because you never knew when "Gone With The Wind" might run on Turner Classic Movies and set her off again.

Art fuelled Aunt Louise's aspirations. She'd linger dreamingly over pictures of Versailles in a coffee table book, then affect a French accent and put doilies woven of lace and gold on every surface in her house. She watched "The Great Gatsby" and made us all show up for Thanksgiving dinner wearing tuxedos and sequined gowns. And then, during that very Thanksgiving dinner with the radio playing (she couldn't actually afford a jazz combo), Aunt Louise heard the Christmas song "Santa Baby".

Eartha Kitt sang: "Santa Baby, slip a sable under the tree, for me."

"Uh oh." I thought.

"Uh oh." whispered my mother.

"Pass the gravy." said my father.

Aunt Louise began to sway in time to Eartha Kitt's sultry voice.

Santa baby, just slip a sable under the tree

For me

Been an awful good girl

Santa baby, so hurry down the chimney tonight

And she was away! Aunt Louise listened intently as Eartha Kitt asked seductively for all SORTS of material treasures. A '54 convertible, a yacht, the deed to a platinum mine, a duplex with cheques endorsed by Santa Claus, Christmas tree decorations from Tiffany's, and, of course, a ring. Eartha Kitt promised to wait up for "Santa cutie" who was going to "hurry down the chimney". The sexual allusions were clear and the exchange offered couldn't have been any more obvious. Eartha Kitt sold Santa Claus as the ultimate lover bearing ridiculously expensive gifts in return for physical affection. And Aunt Louise was hooked.

Santa Mike was first.

I was 14 years old. Now, at 14, a teenaged male has absolutely zero interest in being dragged from mall to mall, visiting Santas as his aunt's wingman while she's on the make. But I had been raised with a strong sense of family duty, so when Aunt Louise informed me that we were going to "make a day of it", I reluctantly nodded and piled into her rusty brown Chevette. As we drove towards the first mall, the magnitude of our undertaking suddenly struck me and my adolescent spirit discovered religion as I prayed to every deity imaginable that cute Bernadette Charbonne from my science class wouldn't spot me.

Zeus, it turns out, must listen to prayers. Because I got through the entire day undetected by any of my peers.

If there is a hell, and I don't really see the need for it now, it involves sitting on the lap of a mall Santa while your 40-something aunt flaunts her slightly leathery cleavage to the poor minimum-wage-paid, toddler-urine-soaked man in the red suit.

After an initial "Ho! Ho! Ho!", Aunt Louise leaned in and introduced herself to Santa. "I'm… Louise" she purred breathily. "Like Tina *Louise* from Gilligan's Island." Santa lowered his voice, afraid of being caught, but equally afraid of giving Louise an excuse to make a scene. "Mike." he whispered. "My real name is Mike." He raised his voice and addressed me.

"And what do you want for Christmas little… erm, young man?"

"Death" came to mind. But I mumbled something about a new bike.

Then Aunt Louise chirped a few of the words to "Santa Baby" to her poor, bearded captive.

I'll wait up for you dear

Santa baby, so hurry down the chimney tonight

The attendant elf snapped a picture of me looking disinterested, Santa looking even more disinterested, and Louise making sure that her left hand, noticeably free of a wedding ring, was right in front of Santa's jolly red nose.

Santa wasn't reading the cues. Or perhaps he was.

"So," said Aunt Louise "how do you keep warm at the North Pole?"

Santa Mike responded distractedly "Oh, you know. Elves."

Aunt Louise grew bolder "Is there a Mrs. Claus?"

Santa Mike figured it out. Then he panicked.

At full volume, Santa Mike exclaimed "HO! HO! HO! I'll see you on Christmas Eve! Now don't forget to eat your vegetables and do what your mother tells you to do."

"She's my aunt, not my mother," I grumbled sullenly.

"HO! HO! HO!" boomed Santa Mike. "And how old are you, Timmy?"

"My name's William." I muttered. "And I'm 14."

Santa Mike paused. Then he whispered to me. "Do you have an older brother, kid?"

The light went on for me.

The light was already on for Santa Mike.

Aunt Louise was clueless. She wanted that '54 convertible too, light blue. She began to sing again.

Think of all the fun I've missed

Think of all the fellas that I haven't kissed

Santa Mike leaned over to Aunt Louise. "Yeah, me too lady. Now take the kid and beat it. Don't forget to pay for the picture." He raised his voice "AND HAVE A VERY MERRY CHRISTMAS!"

The light finally went on for Aunt Louise and she dragged me from Santa Mike's chair. I felt awful. Santa Mike was clearly a nice guy on all counts and here was Aunt Louise making it all weird for him. And me. Mostly me.

She spoke not a word… And we moved quickly through the mall, out to the parking lot, and clambered back into Aunt Louise's embarrassingly awful Chevette. A quick drive to the west side of town and we were at the second mall. The visit to Santa's Grotto was short. Shorter than you'd have thought, but even my desperate and "Santa Baby" obsessed Aunt Louise knew that this was not the Santa for her when he belched a mixture of beer and Thai food into our faces. Moving on.

Santa Chad was next.

We found Santa Chad at the newest of our town's three malls. He was about Aunt Louise's age (I could see salt and pepper hair underneath his wig) and he responded playfully to her clumsy and song-based flirting.

Louise sang:

Come and trim my Christmas tree

With some decorations bought at Tiffany's

I really do believe in you

Let's see if you believe in me

Santa Chad smiled underneath his nylon weave beard and said "Oh, I do. I DO believe!" I was very quickly beginning to feel like a third wheel in their little Yuletide passion play and so, when I saw the opportunity, I slipped away from Santa Chad, leaving him to flirt with Aunt Louise.

Me? I sidled over to the photo elf and hit on her. But a much older woman wanted nothing to do with a 14-year-old adolescent. She was 16. Probably into high school seniors. So, shot down, I trudged towards the mall exit. When Aunt Louise caught up with me, she was singing again and seemed to be skipping.

Santa baby, forgot to mention one little thing

A ring

I don't mean on the phone

Santa baby, so hurry down the chimney tonight

Hurry down the chimney tonight

Aunt Louise stopped and pinched my cheeks.

Hurry, tonight.

Faster than you could say "Dash away, dash away, dash away all", Aunt Louise and Santa Chad were dating. In fact, they became quite the item very quickly. Chad was clearly smitten and Aunt Louise was living out her Christmastime fairy tale.

14 is an awkward age. My older brother, Gerry, was allowed to stay out all night. Dad assumed that Gerry was at some girl's house. Mom and I knew better and merely rolled our eyes. Gerry's awesome. Really, Gerry is the best older brother a guy could have. But he wasn't at "some girl's house", that's for sure. But, despite my protestations, at 14 I wasn't allowed to stay home alone when Mom and

Dad went out for the evening. I had to go and stay with Aunt Louise.

Since Mom and Dad had a lot of social obligations during the Christmas season, I got to spend a lot of nights at Aunt Louise's house and a lot of time with Aunt Louise. And Santa Chad.

They would make sure that I was tucked up in bed (their words) as early as nine o'clock. This was the ultimate indignity to a 14-year-old. Christ, at home, I could stay up until 11, even midnight on some Saturdays. But at Aunt Louise's, bedtime was nine pm. For all of us, it seemed. At nine o'clock, the doors would close, the lights would dim, and the music would start.

Still obsessed with the song, Aunt Louise would play "Santa Baby" on repeat until her bedsprings upstairs began to squeak in time to the music. Meanwhile, I lay in the guest bedroom downstairs, horrified.

Santa Chad had what is known as a "dad bod". A hairy chest with a pot belly. How do I know this? Santa Chad had a habit of pooping with the bathroom door open. Quite a sight at seven am when you're a bleary-eyed teen who's barely awake and wants nothing more in the world than to quickly pee and go back to bed without seeing THAT!

But, bathroom quirks aside, Santa Chad was a genuinely good guy. He very quickly fell in love with my Aunt Louise. He treated me like one-half nephew and one-half buddy. I have many fond memories of snow fort building and general winter goofing off with Santa Chad who, periodically, would then get dressed in the red and white suit and roar off to the mall in his pickup truck for another shift, making magic for the families of our town.

Christmas was coming. And Aunt Louise, convinced that she had found her golden goose, was dropping hints fast and furious. She would traipse about the house, clad in semi-modest lingerie, singing:

> *Santa baby, I wanna yacht*
>
> *And really that's not a lot*
>
> *Been an angel all year*
>
> *Santa baby, so hurry down the chimney tonight*
>
> *Santa honey, one little thing I really need*
>
> *The deed*
>
> *To a platinum mine*
>
> *Santa baby, so hurry down the chimney tonight*

Santa Chad, that poor bastard, had no clue that she really wanted these things or that she thought that he was going to be the ticket to getting them all. Santa Chad, you see, was the one thing that Aunt Louise had never encountered in her life. Santa Chad was an actual artist. An actor. Chad Humphries - I had spotted his picture on a poster for a Bijou Theater production of "Death of a Salesman" - was Santa Claus only during the holiday season. The rest of the time, as he told me, but apparently not Aunt Louise, Santa Chad eked out a living doing community theatre and shooting bit parts in TV series and movies of the week a few towns over from ours. Santa Chad had actually committed his life to making the entertainment magic that enthralls people or, if you're like Aunt Louise, twists their perception of reality beyond recognition. Fortunately for the world at large, there are very few Aunt Louises.

But it was that genuine commitment to magic that made Santa Chad the perfect boyfriend for Aunt Louise. He indulged her fantasies (at 14, I did not fully comprehend what indulging fantasies might include), and he was charmed by her innocence and voracious appreciation for art. Santa Chad had no idea that he was dealing with a total wingnut.

So, inspired by his lover's singing and the most wonderful time of the year, Santa Chad saved his meagre mall Santa earnings and set out in the third week of December to literally "slip a sable under the tree." He travelled from vintage shop to antique store desperately searching for a sable stole or jacket or wrap. Anything sable. He finally found what he was looking for in BonaVista Vintage where an enthusiastic salesman named Justin dug a sable wrap out of a back room. Santa Chad was delighted! And he was certain that this gift would be just the romantic gesture that would steal, and seal, his love's heart as his own.

Then came Christmas morning.

Santa Chad had stayed over at Aunt Louise's. I was in the guest room. Mom and Dad had gone to his mother's for Christmas Eve, and I had developed a sudden stomach ache directly connected to the anticipation of spending Christmas Eve, or even five minutes, in the company of my grandmother, Beatrice. She had given me toy cars for my 14th birthday. I traded them to an eighth grade boy for his father's collection of girly magazines.

Christmas morning dawned and the three of us, Santa Chad, Aunt Louise, and I, converged in the living room around the Christmas tree. We munched on cinnamon buns and drank copious amounts of hot cocoa. Then it was time to open our gifts. Aunt Louise squealed orgasmically as she unwrapped her very own sable wrap. Just like in the song, Santa Baby had slipped a sable under the tree, and Aunt Louise was in heaven. Life, for her, was finally, fully imitating art. She modelled the wrap, twirling and flipping it, savouring the warmth and luxuriating in the pure beauty of the garment. I know it's not fashionable to say so now, but it really was a beautiful fur wrap. And it was vintage, so, frankly, the animals were long dead, and Aunt Louise had nothing to feel guilty for. Not like she would have anyway.

But as the morning wore on, Aunt Louise's mood darkened. Gift after gift, there were no convertible keys, no yacht, no deed to a mine, no duplex, no cheques, no decorations on the tree from Tiffany, and no ring. Aunt Louise was beginning to feel cheated. Santa Chad was, after all, the real Santa Baby, wasn't he? Santa Chad, luckily, didn't seem to notice the black cloud gathering over Aunt Louise's head, so when he went cheerily out into the cold to the only open store in town to fetch some coffee cream, Aunt Louise took the opportunity to corner me.

"What is this all about?"

"Huh?" I said.

"He got the sable. But the rest of the song. We're in the song. We're doing the song!" she protested.

"Ummm... the sable's nice." I offered, weakly.

"But, but... it's like he's a fraud. Like he's pretending." she argued.

"Well, Aunt Louise, what do you want? The sable's a really generous gift from an actor."

"From a... WHAT?!?" she gasped.

"An actor. Chad, Santa Chad, is an actor."

"He's a what?" asked Aunt Louise as if inquiring about an alien life form.

"He's an actor. He pretends to be Santa Claus. Next week he'll be pretending to be Willy Loman, the week after that, he'll be a man in a phone booth on a TV series. That's his job."

"An... actor. He acts?" said Aunt Louise, disbelievingly.

"Yeah, cool huh?" I replied, not comprehending that Aunt Louise was, for that brief moment, looking behind the screen, peering into the magician's hat, and losing every illusion that kept her fragile psyche afloat.

Aunt Louise retreated to a chair and nursed a hot cocoa. Santa Chad came back in from the cold, and she barely spoke to him. Mom and Dad came to pick me up and she saw me to the door and patted me on the head. I paused, sensing that something was off.

"You gonna be okay?" I asked.

"Huh?" said Aunt Louise, distractedly. "Oh, yeah. It's just time to break the spell."

I had no idea what she meant. And so I trudged off to my parents' car to return to the comfort of my own home for gift unwrapping and turkey eating.

Unbeknownst to any of us, Aunt Louise spent the bulk of the day in relative silence, only speaking to Santa Chad when she had to or when "cued" as she would put it to him. She ate sugarplums, claiming she'd dreamed of them the night before, she consumed figgy pudding, mumbling that after all the singing, she bloody well deserved it, then she and Santa Chad sat down to a humble, but tasty Christmas dinner of roasted chicken, stuffing, and gravy. As soon as dinner was finished, Aunt Louise mixed herself a drink and put a Dean Martin Christmas CD into her stereo. She turned it up loud. She sang along with the woman's part of the duet. Santa Chad watched, mutely, as she rose from her seat, drink in hand, and slipped into her prized fur Christmas present.

I really can't stay

I've got to go away

This evening has been so very nice

My mother will start to worry
My father will be pacing the floor

So really I'd better scurry
But maybe just a half a drink more

The neighbors might think
Say what's in this drink?

I wish I knew how
To break this spell

I ought to say, no, no, no sir
At least I'm gonna say that I tried

I really can't stay

Santa Chad caught on and, as the door slammed, he sang one plaintive line to his darling Louise.

But baby, it's COLD OUTSIDE!

We found Aunt Louise in the morning outside the Bijou Theater.

She was clutching a French 75 in her hand, wearing her sable stole, and had an enigmatic Mona Lisa smile on her frozen face.

WHEN CHRISTMAS JUMPED THE SHARK

Two days before Christmas, it was snowing and cold. In a Norman Rockwell print or a Currier and Ives painting, the snow would have been a picturesque blessing. In some places, however, it was life-threatening.

Vancouver, British Columbia, perched on the coast in a Pacific rainforest, is not used to getting snow. But for a few days before Christmas, Vancouver had transformed into a winter wonderland as more than a foot of dry, cold snow fell on the trees, lawns, and rooftops. Ever responsive, the city's snowplows had been busy sitting silently in the yard as the ice and snow piled up on them. A few salt trucks had made it into service and only managed to make the icy city streets worse. Those streets were covered by a carefully measured soup of ice, snow, and salt – crafted by city chemists to ensure maximum slipperiness.

The unused bicycle lanes, however, were expertly cleared by Bobcat shovels and salted by platoons of city workers.

It goes without saying that virtually nobody was stupid enough to ride a bicycle in minus 10.

Pedestrians, however, were active, seemingly engaged in a contest to see what clothing made them the least visible. Was it all black? Was it all white? I had examples of each dash out in front of me on icy roads. They couldn't have been more invisible without a Harry Potter invisibility cloak. And The Hudson's Bay department store was all sold out of those.

It was into that fray that a man with a long white beard and a moustache dashed on foot across one of the city's major streets against the light. I hit the brakes, steered out of the inevitable skid, and swore at Santa Claus.

But I saved Christmas.

And I'm proud of that, naturally. However, the question remains, SHOULD I be proud of that?

Shortly after I nearly killed Father Christmas, I wandered into a store to shop for stocking stuffers. I found the usual trinkets – cookie cutters and twinkle lights and stupid ties with reindeer on them (sorry, "National Lampoon"). As I shopped, I reflected that Christmas had slipped into dangerous territory.

There is an expression in showbiz that something has "jumped the shark". It refers to the moment in a project's existence when everyone has run out of ideas and resorts to doing something so monumentally ridiculous as to beggar belief. The expression comes from a beloved sitcom of the 1970s, "Happy Days". In that series, bereft of any further quality ideas, the producers decided that an episode would focus on a main character's attempt to literally jump over a shark on water skis. It was absurd and gave rise to a standing expression that a series, movie, play, or any project has done something utterly bonkers and "jumped the shark".

In 2022, I believe that Christmas "jumped the shark".

Why? As I've said before, I'm not terribly religious. I'm a little too old for full buy-in to Santa Claus. But I enjoy Christmas. In fact, I revere Christmas in my own way. I am by no means a purist. Christmas was created for people to have fun, express themselves in unique ways, form and celebrate connections, decorate trees, bake cookies, maybe pray, maybe sing.

It was not made for beard ornaments.

For what? I can actually hear you saying it.

Beard ornaments.

Beard ornaments are a thing. They are, literally, bauble ornaments that clip into someone's beard. It was 2022, so hipsters had still not been hunted to extinction (as of this writing, I remain hopeful) and men with long beards were still a thing despite women

with good taste letting them know over and over that men with long beards were non-sexy.

Which is okay. Because if someone's beard is long enough to hang beard ornaments in, I'm pretty happy for them to remove themselves from the pursuit of reproduction.

How do I know about beard ornaments? I saw a package of them in a famous drug store that shall remain nameless but that is named after the capital city of England. Then I saw another package. Beard ornaments were actually on sale and I wondered quietly if the dinosaurs had invented them before being wiped off the face of the planet. The timing would seem about right.

"Hey, T-Rex?"

"Yeah, Stegosaurus?"

"Look at this! I have beard ornaments!"

"WHOA, COOL! Where did you get... hey, is that a comet?"

Let's ignore the reality that dinosaurs didn't celebrate Christmas and almost certainly did not have beards. If they did, and if they developed beard ornaments, it was definitely time for them to go.

I stood staring at the packages of festive decorations for facial hair. I knew one thing for sure, beard ornaments were going to be sold to unsexy men with unsexy beards who would then have unsexy baubles. The only thing that these men would be waking up to on Christmas morning was the sound of the door slamming as their girlfriends moved home to their parents.

I chuckled sadistically.

That's when a hipster with a beard pushed rudely past me and grabbed a package. I stared at him.

"What?" he challenged me.

"Um, nothing. Just curious to see who actually buys these."

"Whatever. You judgy old bastard."

At 57, I really don't think that I qualify as "old", but when you're twentysomething and about to adorn yourself with beard baubles, I guess everyone seems old.

I gave him my broadest Yuletide smile and called out effusively "MERRY CHRISTMAS!" Then added, "Tiny Tim."

He grimaced and headed for the checkout.

I shrugged. It was official. There really are beard ornaments, people to buy them, and Christmas is ruined.

I stumbled out into the snow. Bracing myself against the ice-covered fender of my car as the frozen flakes whipped my face, my destiny in the face of Yuletide beard baubles became clear.

I got into my Ford Explorer and turned the ignition. Slowly, I maneuvered out of the parking lot. I cruised along the city streets, caked with snow, slush, and ice.

It took a while, but finally Jolly Old St. Nicholas, with his white beard and moustache, dashed out from between two parked cars.

This time, I didn't miss.

Credits

Greg Leach: Illustrator

Tom Carter: Cover Colourist and Title Designer

Greg Dixon: Layout, Organisation, Digital Experience Edition, Audio Readings